the chamber within

KT Finegan

Rebecca Perkin spent many years writing and re-writing *White Plains*. It was a love/hate relationship but one she will always be glad to have embarked upon. Having studied illustration at university she has always been creative, but it is writing that pushes her forward and gives her purpose in this world.

To keep updated and be the first to know when Rebecca's books are released, please visit: www.rebeccaperkinauthor.com

You can sign up to her newsletter for exclusives, giveaways, competitions and more!

You can also follow her on twitter @RebeccaPerkin

the chamber within

KT Finegan

Betty Books

Published in 2018 by Betty Books

ISBN Paperback: 978-0-9955000-2-0
Ebook: 978-0-9955000-3-7

A CIP catalogue copy of this book can be found in the British Library.

Published with the help of Indie Authors World
indieauthorsworld.com

To my dad, William Oliver Finegan, I love you always

Acknowledgements:

Thanks to Kim and Sinclair MacLeod at Indie Authors World, and to the magic community of indie authors they have created, I appreciate all your support. The tea and biscuits are also always welcome. A special thank you to fellow writer Alice Graham for reading and editing the early drafts of The Chamber Within, and for joining me in our mission to find good cakes. To my sister Elizabeth, niece Eli and nephew Oli, thanks for putting up with me again. My dad used to tell me stories about Newgrange where he said he played as a boy. I hope I've captured its essence in this story, and that my Drogheda relatives enjoy it. To all my friends, thank you for supporting me in this second book, and to everyone who contacted me about The Thirteen Stones, and wanted to know more about Kirsty's journey, I really hope you enjoy The Chamber Within.

Chapter One

The sound of silent anticipation filled the old stone chamber as I stood with a hundred other souls. All of us lost in excitement, awaiting the winter solstice sun to appear through a tiny slit in the wall and fill the cavern with dawn light. The way it had for over five thousand years. It was as if I could hear my ancestors whispering in my ear. This was the right place for me. This felt like home.

We stood in reverence to the power of the sun and the ingenuity of Stone Age people, who had built this amazing place by hand from rock and soil, perfectly aligned with their vision of the winter sky. We waited, cameras ready to catch the magic moment of light in this temple to the sun, in deepest Ireland.

We waited. Someone official, perhaps from the tourist organisation who managed the ancient site, finally counted down to the dawn majesty and we stood ready as silent witnesses.

Standing in the darkness towards the back of the monument, I couldn't see a thing. Faintly from outside, I could hear a dull drum beat. Hundreds of people stood there, unable to get inside, like us, ready to welcome the dawn, and the New Year. The shortest day; from now on, more sunlight. Like our ancient ancestors we, too, wanted to see the end of the winter.

The drums reached a pounding rhythmic crescendo, and then there was nothing except an unexpected, unnerving, deathly silence.

There's always that moment when you just know that something isn't right. You can hear it unsaid, an energy, an awareness that grips people. Nothing happened. No sunlight lit the chamber. Some people shuffled, some coughed, no-one spoke. No-one wanted to be the first to spoil the moment, to break the spell that had surrounded us. The special ones feeling so proud. Twenty-first century mystical believers, standing where our forefathers had once stood, celebrating the sun.

And then it happened. Panic. No-one knew what to do. Pushing, pulling, and running in the darkness. Hitting the sharp, rugged stones of the cave. Shouting, trying to reach loved ones. Fear. Screaming. Fuelling more panic. Not knowing where to go, and all thoughts of specialness gone. Instead, primeval survival; perhaps we were closer to our Stone Age ancestors than we had realised.

The crowd ran around as a wild group, hunting for the narrow exit along the tight, low passageway to outside the monument. In haste to get away, and yet not knowing what awaited them.

I felt outside of it all and for some reason they couldn't see me. It was as if I was invisible. And as they all turned to run, screaming in panic that the sun hadn't come up, I was knocked off my feet and fell to the floor. My face forced into the cold, dank ground, I could taste its bitterness. I couldn't shout out with earth in my mouth and nose. I felt the pain of winter boots on my back and head, treading me into the floor of the cavern. Standing on me, kicking me, bruising me, and I felt myself faint. Dropping into darkness, a rushing pulse in my ears, and pain in my body. I felt myself give up. Give in. No oxygen, my nose and mouth filling with soil. I was dying.

I sat up, panting for breath, in the cold, dark air of my childhood bedroom, and it took me a moment to realise I was safe. None of it was real. I was in bed, not in a darkened cave. Slowly, my breathing returned to normal. Sweat had rolled down my neck; my damp hair icy in the pre-dawn chill.

I sat up quickly, then forced myself out of bed with a shudder and shiver as the freezing Scottish winter grabbed me in its tight grasp. Stumbling about in the dark, I was not really clear where I was or even what I was. Fear from the dream hung over me. I banged my freezing toe against something solid. The corner of the bed. My frozen feet sent a scream along the icy nerve pathways to my brain, and in the pain everything rushed back to me. I'd had another nightmare. The same one I'd had for the last few nights. It had been such an unsettling time. First of all the end of a long term relationship, then Gran's unexpected death, and what I'd gone through in finding out what had happened to her. All within the last few weeks, and then my father, missing from my life for such a long time, called to ask for my help, and with that one conversation, I moved from loneliness to having family. It was no wonder I was having strange dreams, nightmares had plagued me all my life, especially when stressed.

Yet it all seemed so ridiculous. For me to be dreaming of Newgrange. A place I didn't know, and only in my head because of that call from my father asking me to help save it. An ancient stone chamber in Ireland built as a temple to the winter sun, and he seemed to think it was in danger of some kind. The thought, more worrying for me, *what exactly did he think I could do?* And here we were, a week or so before the winter solstice celebration, and my nightmares were waking me every night. Since that call across the years and miles, there was nothing else from him. I was now doubting that it was real, perhaps a cruel hoax. I shook my head, this is what I always did. Over analyse and worry, *would I ever stop?*

In the predawn haze of a Scottish winter, I felt for my thick, fleecy dressing gown, instant comfort from its warmth, rammed my feet into sheepskin slippers, and then pulled a tartan, woollen blanket around my shoulders. Scratchy yet familiar as it always carried the scent of home. I ran downstairs, flicked on the kettle, still warm from refilling my hot water bottle hours earlier, and headed quickly to the relative warmth of the stove. My breath steamed in the air around me as I ran through the icy atmosphere, it was as cold as being outside. I used my sleeve to open the metal handle and threw in some firelighters, thin twigs for kindling, and a couple of logs. Closing the glass door again, I knew it would catch light and soon heat the old cottage. Within a few minutes, the kettle had boiled. I hastily made some tea, hopping from foot to foot to warm up and then sat huddled against the fireplace. Breathing heavily from the exertion, I shivered again, my body struggling to warm up in the icy atmosphere.

Flames crackled, logs spat and hissed against the glass as if trying to escape, and their silent shadows danced around the room. The low pale walls glowed red and orange and outside the winter storm relaxed its anger slightly. Thick snow and high winds had been my only visitors for days, and I was finding the prolonged isolation unsettling.

Sitting in my late gran's cottage, left to me as her only living relative, I breathed deeply as I felt her all around me. There was almost a sigh somewhere near my ear. I sensed her moving close as if to comfort me. Breathing deeply again I sat back against the cushions, closed my eyes, and surrendered towards sleep. It was the space where I felt closest to all those I had lost.

I must have dozed off as my head soon filled with images of my grandmother, young and vivacious, laughing, her head thrown back as she ran through a meadow of thigh high grass. Snow topped mountains sat in the distance. A Scotland we both loved. The sun burning bright in the blue sky, she was showing off to me, dancing and twirling her skirts around as she played in the sunshine for an admiring audience of one. I could smell the freshness of the meadow, beautiful lilac forever flowering in the garden of my soul. She put her arms out to me and the clock stopped as I stood enveloped in her embrace. Every cell in my body soothed with the sensation. I could feel her. She whispered something to me. I struggled to hold on to the sound of her voice. In her soft Scottish burr, I heard my name. She faded, faintly, like the scent all around her, I captured one word only "signs". This felt real. This was real, and with that thought another followed quickly behind as I started to wake. She was gone, physically gone, my dreams were only that. With the sadness of recent loss I opened my eyes to a chilly darkness, dawn still hours away, sitting on what I would always think was Granny's chair, the fire almost out, and ice in the air.

It's as well I woke when I did as Scottish winters' were

brutal, and the temperature outside had hovered at minus 10 degrees for the last two weeks, ever since the funeral. As if the whole earth was as chilled as my heart. My breath misted in the air, and as I watched it swirled around in a draught, looking like the figure of a woman dancing. Like Gran was reaching across from my sleep to my waking. The thought of her so near always brought comfort and a little thaw to my heart. However, my body shivered and I had to move so I hurriedly filled the stove up again with logs, kindling and firelighters, no artistry nor skill in my attempt to heat the room. I nudged against it in an attempt to warm up, my mind wandering back to the knowledge I now had of the light after death. Although I'd hardly spoken to anyone since my recent experience deep below the graveyard of the local town, I felt in every part of my body and of my soul that it had been real. And even though it broke every earthly rule, I was sure that I had ventured to hell and back.

I had no idea that I would have to do it all again so soon. Ireland was calling to me in my dreams. Calling me home.

Chapter Two

Sleep again must have found me and I eventually woke a little after nine. It was still dark outside and I was stiff and cold and in desperate need of heat, food and the company of others. The snow was so high outside the isolated cottage I hadn't yet cleared the path or attempted the walk into town. One look through the frost patterned windows, showed that no thaw was imminent. A shelf of snow cloud hung low in the lightening sky, and extravagant icicles decorated every tree, branch and fence. I knew I had to get out. I was bored and so lonely. I had read every book in the cottage and had no internet connection for my laptop. My mobile only picked up a signal at the top of the garden so I hadn't spoken to anyone in days as it was too much of an effort to head outside. Even worse, the aerial on the roof was too heavy with ice and snow so the reception for the old television kept cutting out.

Right after Gran died and I'd returned to Scotland for the funeral, sitting in front of the television during the day had seemed like a treat, a little indulgence in my grief time. Now it felt like torture. I had to get out of the house. The old stone cottage sat at the very edge of town, close to the only graveyard and overlooking the waterfalls which had powered mills centuries before, and were now a world heritage site. Usually the pounding of the water reached me but this icy spell had silenced even that, and I found the strange stillness unsettling. My thoughts kept taking me back to sad times, bitter sweet memories of family, now all gone.

I'd had time to go through my memory box though, and that had yielded mixed results and as usual mixed emotions. I found it tucked away at the back of the deep cupboard in my old bedroom. I'd traced my finger across the childish writing on the cover, instantly taken back decades. Inside I'd found my old primary school tie, some coloured crayons that disintegrated at my touch, and an old silver pendant with a strange symbol picked out in red coloured glass on its surface. And then much to my surprise, at the bottom of the box, I found a stack of letters addressed to me. They were carefully bound by a faded pink ribbon, all were unopened, my name and address at the cottage written out in big bold handwriting. I'd ripped them open to discover years and years of letters and cards, every one full of love, signed by my dad. I cried over and over in the dark bedroom, sitting huddled on the floor, feeling completely alone. I was sure I'd never seen them before. Perhaps Gran had left them for me to discover. After all she'd arranged everything else for me. The cottage was completely cleaned and tidied when I'd arrived, everything organised and put away. Knowing that he had kept in touch meant more than I'd ever thought. I really wanted to meet him again.

Generations of my family had lived and worked from this cottage, and all around me were the remains of their lives in pots and pans, bits and bobs. The wooden floorboards, stripped and stained years before, and covered with a variety of rugs and mats, in every shade of faded colour. I wasn't sure whether I would ever clear any of it away. Gran's death had been so unexpected, and yet with its sadness had ushered in the opportunity to live back in Scotland and leave London and outraged heartbreak behind. Realistically though, I would have to put in some more modern home improvements to make the cottage more liveable. Gran was obviously a hardier soul than I or perhaps even she would have struggled in this biting cold, the coldest spell for fifty years everyone in the town had said. The stove was the only heating, and without an electric shower there was no way I was facing the icy bathroom. Frozen in time as well as temperature, black and white tiles, and a green bath, replaced sometime in the seventies possibly, it was functional although not particularly enticing. At my flat in London we'd had underfloor heating and constant hot water, only when I returned to the cottage did I realise that it had been a sad and soulless place nevertheless. I had wasted far too many nights sitting on my own waiting for me ex to come home. That was before I found him with his secretary.

"Not working." As I explained to my friends. Their affair had lasted for years and I felt a fool when I realised. I shook my head again to shake out the past, why did it creep into my thoughts so easily? Leaving it all behind and coming home felt like the right thing to do, for me though, the betrayal still hurt, and I wished Gran was here to talk it over with, make some scones and drink pots of tea.

Unfortunately, I was almost out of milk and food, so I really needed to get into town. I tentatively washed at the kitchen sink with hot water from the kettle. There was no chance of being seen. Gran had net curtains at every window except the kitchen, it faced onto the small side vegetable garden and wasn't overlooked. Our closest neighbour was miles away across open fields. The postman was likely to be the only visitor, until a thaw and the local farmer cleared the path even he wouldn't get through.

I hopped from one bare foot to another as I pulled on the last of my clean clothes. Teeth chattering I was chilled to the bones as Gran used to say. Dark jeans, fleece top, mismatched socks. I pulled the woollen scarf back around my neck as a muffler and quickly and without care dragged my crazy curly hair into a pony tail of sorts. I used my little hand mirror to help me apply some mascara, and to make sure I didn't have panda eyes from my tears. The last few weeks I hadn't properly cared for myself and I knew that my friends in London would have struggled to recognise my lack of makeup and hairstyling. Always so important in the life I'd left behind, and surprisingly not of much interest since Gran had died. I knew I had to get a grip, at least that's what I kept saying to myself, usually followed with some disappointment and self-criticism as I spent another day at the cottage with unwashed hair avoiding mirrors. It was easier that way.

I desperately needed to do a laundry but there was no way anything would dry in this damp air. The downstairs of the cottage consisted of a large kitchen, opening on to a little lounge area, with Gran's bedroom at the back of the house. The kitchen was painted a sunny yellow which always seemed to glow when the sun lit it up. The main room opening on to the kitchen was where I tended to sit, huddled on Gran's faded chair and close to the stove. Across from it a faded dusky pink velour sofa, along the back she had a lace trimmed cover of some kind. I didn't know what it was for, nor the matching cloth trims that sat over its arms. I knew if I ever took them off the cloth beneath would be lighter. The walls were lined with a pale pink floral patterned wallpaper. Even though the woman who lived here had been bright as a button, I hadn't noticed how faded the house had become over the years, and it suddenly saddened me that I hadn't been here to see it. Up the rugged wooden staircase were two little bedrooms under the eaves. Mine and my mother's, like two little peas in a pod, or so Gran always said. Mine painted pink and the other painted green.

For as long as I remember I told everyone my parents had died when I was young. It now seemed crazy to think that I had told myself that story for so long that I'd believed it. With my grandmother as my only relative, it meant I didn't have to face childhood memories. I had only ever remembered the two of us together, close as anything. These last few weeks had made me look at so much more than Gran's death. Thoughts came unbidden into my mind of Mum dying in a psychiatric hospital, tormented by psychic visions. She didn't want to face what she knew she'd have to, what I'd faced in my turn, and I could understand that now. I was just so sorry that I hadn't been able to help. The girl I was had found it easier to vanish my family instead. It was easier to tell a tale of being alone, and now that felt shameful somehow. Like I needed to have others feel sorry for me than to tell the truth. I knew I'd finally found my family's love, or at least opened myself to receiving it. Yet even now, the physical loss would overwhelm me in powerful waves, followed by the poisoned twins of regret and blame. Finding out that Dad was alive, and that he had been in contact with Gran made me feel more ashamed. How I wish I'd understood more. Gran had done the best by me yet sadness still hung around, and despite my recent experiences I wished so much for another chance with her. A chance with all of them. At Gran's graveyard I had felt so alone, bereft, believing that all my family were gone. Hearing from Dad after all those years opened something in my heart, a tiny flicker of hope. I realised though that my biggest fear was that he wouldn't forgive me for my lack of understanding. For my childhood need to fit in and have a sad story to tell other people. With shame I knew I'd given myself the label of abandoned in my need to feel special.

With my heart full of sadness, I knew I needed to talk to someone. Deciding to walk to the town and the solace of Angel's Cakes, the most amazing coffee shop I'd ever known, I looked forward to the company of others. It even sold angelic gifts, statues, books and music. I'd found some peace in that place, and a couple of new friends as well in the owner Angel and her older friend Grizelle who had gone to school with Gran. I wanted to ask her more about that time and to see if she had any photos. Making up my mind I quickly pulled open the wooden cupboard closest to the door and found an old pair of pink snow boots, with a thick white rubber sole. I would need them to get through the snow, my wedge suede boots were fine for London, not for this country town nor this weather. Neatly lined up on the boot rack I saw Granny's old green wellingtons, her gardening clogs, and her stout brown leather lace up brogues. I sat down and gently touched them, running my finger over the smooth edges, worn down from a lifetime of hard walking across the countryside. The smell of rubber, leather and earth reached me, full of memories of her in the garden, and of other snow filled days. For so long it was only the two of us, we'd had such an amazing bond. She more than made up for any losses I knew that deep inside me. She made me feel like the centre of her world. It was her way. She made everyone feel like that. Always so connected to everyone and everything, including the very earth we stood upon. She loved the town and the country itself with a passion I'd yet to find for anything. Distracted with my sadness, I was struggling into my thick down filled coat when a loud knock hit the kitchen door. I jumped in fright and squealed out, my hand instinctively covering my mouth. The snow had muffled any sounds of footsteps. Given my recent experiences I was unnerved, as I had never spent even one night alone in the cottage before her death. Gran had always been at home for me. I was in yet another moment of loss, and stood a moment, trying to compose myself, taking slow breaths deep into my body. I closed my eyes, trying to find a place of calm in spite of my racing pulse. Someone knocked loudly again, urgently, as I stretched over to reach the door. A recent memory flashed into my mind. The kitchen in disarray, dark, supernatural forces at work. A five-sided star thrown on the floor in salt. The only word in my mind was protection. I dismissed it immediately in my rush to open the door before it banged again. I hadn't learned at that time how to work with my intuition. Given what happened later, how I wish I had.

"Are you in Kirsten?" what I thought was a child's voice called. "It's me"

I took a moment to compose myself. Only a little girl, looking for Gran, not for me. With a deeper sigh, I unlocked and pulled open the solid wooden door. Snow fell in over my boots, and I was temporarily dazzled by the brightness from all around. Grey snow cloud sat low in the sky above us. Old people in the town would say that more was still to come. The storm had been crazy, thunder, lightning and a snow blizzard.

A spark of blue light flashed at the edge of my vision and that whisper again in my mind

"…signs…"

A dark shadow fell across me, and I could not stop a slight shiver throughout my body, as if it knew before my mind did that trouble was coming. My heart lurched in my chest, and yet I felt compelled to open the door as if I deserved my fate. The one thought in my head, like a little voice nagging me was that with all my recent experiences, *how bad could this be?*

Chapter Three

Relief flooded through me immediately. I looked down to see a tiny woman standing on the step and she coughed nervously. Dressed in a bright red coat, with a yellow woollen hat pulled low over her ears, and a matching scarf tight around her neck. She reminded me of a little elf from a childhood fairy tale, and she was almost thigh deep in snow. Forcing her way up my uncleared lane and garden path must have been exhausting, and I immediately felt guilty. After all I hadn't even tried to leave the house in days, and hadn't attempted to clear the path. Gran would never have left it like that. Admiration flowed through me, she was such a strong old character. Another involuntary shiver brought me back to my unexpected visitor. The air was so chilled our breaths met in the air between us.

"Eh hello….. I was looking for Kirsten?"

She looked at me and then looked away again. Nervously licking her lips, and rubbing her woollen gloved hands together.

"I've got an appointment".

I still hadn't said anything, and I realised I was struggling to say the words.

"My gran passed away two weeks ago." My voice broke. Pain came from nowhere. An excruciating physical pain in my heart so unexpected I couldn't breathe for it. I covered my eyes and then started to cry. "She's gone...."

The woman put out her arms and hugged me as she turned me back into the kitchen. Shutting the door behind us and pulling out one of Gran's old kitchen chairs, it screeched across the flagstone floor like chalk down a blackboard. I sat sobbing. *Where had all this emotion come from? As someone who had rarely cried, when would this stop? When would I be able to speak about her death without breaking down?* A pain throbbed in my head and my eyes burned. Within a few moments it passed and I watched as she shrugged off her red coat to reveal a matching red sweater. So bright and colourful and a complete contrast against my black clothes. She seemed to know her way around Gran's kitchen though, and found the tea things, and the last of the custard creams. My least favourite biscuit, so they'd been safe at the back of the cupboard where Gran must have left them. That started the tears again. I sniffed as she popped a mug in front of me on the wooden kitchen table, and my hand reached out to the biscuits automatically.

"I'm Jane. I'm so sorry for your loss and for upsetting you. I had no idea she had gone. She usually gets in touch with me to confirm our appointments but I hadn't heard anything, and then I had a funny dream last night about her, and I knew I had to come. I am so sorry to upset you. ...these were her favourites."

And she gestured towards the crumbs on the table, and burst into tears. It was my turn to try and comfort her. I hated to see another person in distress. It killed me.

"It's ok. Please don't cry you'll start me off again. It's the shock, that's all. Come on, you'll be fine."

It was a surreal scene in a kitchen that had witnessed

many extraordinary moments. I closed my eyes for a moment and felt Gran come closer to me, like she was there with me, holding me safe. Nudging a memory out of me. I opened the top dresser drawer and found one of Gran's little white handkerchiefs from where they were always kept, and the sight of it had us both in tears again. I turned and popped on the still warm kettle. Despite her strange appearance on this freezing cold day, I was warming to her. She looked like she was suffering and her tears showed that she missed Gran too, I told myself.

"Gran passed away two weeks ago. I'm sorry I didn't know you had an appointment with her or I would have tried to get in touch with you. Have you come far? It's a terrible day to be out. The snow has been heavy for weeks but I was thinking of going into town I need some things."

And some company, I thought, the words remained in my head.

"Can you tell me what it was about? Maybe I could help?"

I seriously doubted it. *I mean what on earth could she have wanted with my gran?* I had always thought of her as a slightly eccentric old lady interested in herbal remedies, crystals and angels. Since her death I realised that she was much more than that, she had helped so many people in the town. And recently I discovered, that in death, she had helped a lot more. More than anyone would ever know.

Jane was tiny, less than five foot tall, with long glossy black hair. As she sat across from me, sipping her tea, she closed her eyes, as if savouring the moment. She was a lot older than I'd thought at first. And there was something odd about her. I couldn't put my finger on it. It was something in the way she sat, taking everything in, or perhaps it was the way she spoke, in her high singsong voice, with her head turned at a little angle. Something in the way she glanced around the kitchen, with her huge blue eyes, long lashes and thick brows, like she was looking for something. I was still learning how to listen to my instincts, my intuition. A wise friend of Gran's had told me to breathe deeply and go within my body before I made decisions. And in doing that, as I sat there watching her, something was trying to catch my attention.

"She was showing me how to make em…. remedies and things…' she whispered. I've been coming to see her for the last six months, she said she wanted to show me how to make…"

"Remedies and things?" I finished for her.

She giggled and I would have joined in except for the sudden draft that appeared from nowhere, chilling me deep into my heart. I shivered again and pulled my scarf closer around me. An unbidden thought came to mind, what was it Gran used to say? "Like someone walking over your grave?" I shivered again, and used that as an excuse to jump up to fill the stove, feeling so much better with some distance between us. As I walked back to join Jane at the kitchen table I knew that this visit was significant in some way. Gran came into my mind. What was she'd said to me in that dream this morning? "…signs…. watch for signs."

Jane's sudden appearance in this snow when not even the postman had managed it, could be a sign. Of what? I shivered again, and felt suddenly sickly. Something wasn't right about this day, biting that thought back, I smiled at her reassuringly, she seemed upset about Gran's death and because of that I felt I could trust her.

"Where have you come from?" I asked. Gran's work was still a bit of a mystery to me and I needed a bit of time to work through what this woman had said already. Very recently I'd been introduced to angels, through another of Gran's friends. For someone who was a complete non believer, the concept of a spiritual world really had challenged me. However, the feeling of love and acceptance I'd felt when she helped me connect was like nothing I'd ever experienced. In the last week, stuck in the cottage I had started to wonder if it had been some sort of hallucination. It hadn't happened again. Sitting across the table from this woman, I sensed a need for comfort and sent out a silent SOS to help me stay strong and understand whatever I had to learn from this experience. I immediately felt better, and my breathing deepened and slowed.

"I came from Glasgow, a place called Temple."

"Temple? Really? Now that's a significant place name. How did you get here today? In this snow? I'd assumed that the trains were off "

She shrugged, and her blue eyes almost glowed. "It wasn't too bad a journey. I knew I had to come."

At the time I missed that she hadn't really answered me.

"Temple….? What's it like? How did it get its name?"

"It's on the main road heading west out of the city" she said. "It's close to where they found a Druids Temple. Sometime in the 1930s. But they built a road over it before the Second World War."

"Seriously! That's crazy, why would they do that?" I felt indignant for some reason.

Her large eyes widened and she sipped her tea, saying nothing.

"It's funny I'm sure I've heard about this from someone fairly recently. A Druid's Temple in Glasgow? How old was it? Weren't the Druid's around years and years ago?"

"Possibly five thousand years ago. It predates Stonehenge."

"No way!" And the thought that someone had built a road over it felt unfair to me, unfair and short sighted.

"It's true, it was uncovered by an archaeologist from one of the universities in Glasgow. Although the Temple was covered over in the 1930s, I think the place held some sort of energy. If you believe in that?" Her question warmed the air between us, I was transfixed. It seemed so incredible yet felt so true. "I heard that young mothers in the area used to push crying babies in their prams along the road, to quieten them down."

"As if they knew it was magic." We both said together, and laughed.

"Is it still there? Do you think I could find it?" I asked.

"It's behind a petrol station on the main road out of Glasgow the Great Western Road, on the road to Clydebank. Here I'll write down the name, you can't miss it. Would you be driving?"

"I don't have a car here yet. I moved back from London after the funeral." I told her as I slipped the note into my pocket, "So probably the train or bus. I'm sure I'll find it. I feel I have to go. I don't know why…"

"If you are getting the bus get off after the retail park, and you'll see what remains of the wee river, funny I was thinking that it runs into the River Clyde on the other side of Glasgow, and here we are where the river starts. That's amazing don't you think?" said Jane looking away from me, almost like someone else was talking to her. As if I wasn't there. "You should follow your gut instinct. That's what your Gran always said. I learned so much from her. She really was special."

"Thanks. I know and lots of people have said that to me. It means a lot. How did you meet her? I love to hear these stories."

"We were introduced by some mutual friends" she said. There was something about the way she looked as she spoke that caught my attention. She didn't look directly at me, instead her eyes looked way past, and then darted around the room. Something didn't ring true, but I hadn't learned then to tune into those little signs. I missed it and the moment passed. I concentrated on what she said, not how she said it and how that made me feel.

Jane took a deep breath, and tucked her hair behind her ears, she leaned towards me with a shy smile and asked to see Gran's journals, her precious red books passed down from family members, full of what I always thought of as recipes. Women in our family had written in them going back years.

In my usual urgency to please I immediately agreed and jumped up in a rush to find them on the first shelf of the walk-in cupboard Granny called her "press". It was behind a door at the back of the kitchen. In fact if you didn't know it was there, you'd probably miss it given it matched perfectly the wooden panelling on the wall. It had floor to ceiling wide wooden shelves full of glass jars and bottles, all neatly labelled with Gran's neat and tiny handwriting. I had forgotten about the mysteries of this cupboard. It had mesmerised me as a child. I had forgotten of the reverence and respect that Gran had always shown to the contents. She called it her treasure and would never open it when anyone else was in the house. She insisted that visitors sit near the fire, and then would slip into the press to find "something special" to help with an illness or ailment. Here I was opening it in front of a stranger. I shivered at that thought, after all Jane was a friend of Gran's wasn't she? A little flash of light caught the edge of my vision. I knew it was some sort of sign, not what it meant.

Gran was always cooking or baking from a recipe from one of her red books lying open in the middle of the big pine kitchen table. With the cupboard door opened I could smell ginger and nutmeg, cinnamon and mint. It took me back to happy times, giggling and laughing with her, the radio on in the background, and a little pang of longing for Gran pierced my heart.

Jane held out her hands for the books, her eyes twinkled with what I thought was recognition and excitement. She quickly flicked through the first as if she was looking for something. "Look this is one of your family remedies for manifesting a new love" she said.

Eh what?

"I know it probably sounds mad, but Kirsten had all kinds of "remedies". She was a keeper of secrets, wasn't she, like a …..guardian?" She dropped her gaze back to the tea, and her question sat like a wall between us.

How could I possibly begin to tell this woman what I knew of Gran's guardianship? How could I begin to tell her of the knowledge I now held that interrupted my dreams? I couldn't. The moment passed and again a sense of unease slowly spread deep inside my stomach. I was aware of a sudden darkness outside and thunder rumbled, I shivered. Something wasn't right and it was as if even the weather was trying to catch my attention.

"So do you know what to use to get rid of a waster husband… or wife?"

Her question came out of nowhere, and I laughed to try to break the tension, and yet I could tell by the way she looked at me that she was serious. As much as I was really interested, I tried to keep the conversation light and over the next hour or so Jane talked me through some of the things Gran had shown her. Remedies from natural herbs and plants, for coughs and colds, and all sorts of other ailments.

I mentioned the weather conditions a few times in the hope that she'd take the hint and leave, she was unconcerned, and kept returning to the journals, finding more and more recipes of interest to her.

I jumped in fright with a particularly loud boom of thunder and lightning flash and the lights in the cottage flickered. I was unnerved again and really wanted Jane to go. There was a part of me that wanted to be alone with my sadness, and yet another part of me that enjoyed the company. I realised that all I could do was go with my strongest feeling, and that was for Jane to leave. I did want companionship, but I wanted good friends and support, not a very strange stranger.

"This has been really interesting Jane, I really need to get into town before the storm worsens. Why don't we walk back together and you can get the train, in case they are cancelled?" Again I smiled at her and pulled a face, rubbing my tummy "I'd like to get some food today and don't want to leave it too late."

There was a strange expression on her face and for a second I actually thought she was going to refuse. A loud bang at the door interrupted the moment. It was quickly followed by more knocking and breathing so loud I could hear each rasp and rattle. We exchanged a concerned glance as the handle turned and the door was thrown open so forcefully it crashed against the wall. I had no time to call out as a fleeting thought flashed through my mind of the books lying on the table. Gran treasured them and I hadn't. Was someone coming to steal them?

In the low doorway of my little cottage, blocking out the light, stood a red bearded man. His eyes dark and hidden beneath a black cap pulled low over his brows, green tartan scarf wrapped around his neck, with a heavy dark coat buttoned tight to his chin. He looked as surprised to see us as we him. I took a step back, across the stone floor, the back of my foot hitting the chair leg so I knew I couldn't retreat any further. I was grateful for Jane's presence behind me. His breath rasped in his chest and he coughed loudly into his scarf, turning away from us as he did so. He brought with him the smell of outside, of pine and snow, damp and cold, and very strong body odour, like he hadn't washed for weeks.

"I was looking for Kirsten?" He growled. Then he must have noticed our expressions and he added "I 'm sorry. I've lost my voice….. lost my way…. lost my heart" and with that his eyes filled with tears and he turned away from us in shame, shielding his eyes with his gloved hands. A loud cough bent him double and I realised it explained the heavy breathing. He wasn't well.

Relief and compassion flooded through me. Despite his appearance he was harmless. Simply full of cold and heartache, and I knew what that felt like. For the second time that day, I gestured for a stranger to enter the kitchen, and switched on the kettle again. I smiled a little to myself as

I found another mug and waved him over to the kitchen table. I knew Gran would have loved this, and I knew she would also know I was well out of my comfort zone.

"Please join us". I said "You must be looking for Gran… She's not here… any more."

He looked a little surprise as he took in the kitchen behind me, then his eyes filled with tears again. "My name is Andy Campbell. I live across the valley there. I've had flu for weeks, so I haven't been around much. What happened?"

Why did people always do that? Asking the recently bereaved for details of the death. As if it really mattered. My irritation at his question meant I didn't get as upset as I had earlier.

"She passed away recently". It was all I could say. I focused on filling the teapot, shrugging off any more explanation, and nodded back behind me towards the table, hoping he'd just come in and close the door. I had hoped Jane would have helped at this point. Even as I turned to look at where she had sat I had the strangest feeling, and a little shiver ran down my spine. She was gone.

And so were Granny's journals.

Chapter Four

All that was left on the table was the mug I'd been drinking from and some crumbs from the biscuit packet. Jane if that's what she was called, had disappeared. Along with any sign that she'd ever sat there with me. More shockingly though, the books had gone, Gran's pride and joy, my family's legacy. Gone. I felt like a fool, shame and anger overtook the blood pulsing in my veins, as I tore through the house calling her name. I was terrified that she had indeed vanished, and I was also a little scared that she hadn't. That I'd got this all wrong, and was making a fool of myself. That I'd be embarrassed when she returned to the room.

My heart beat threatened to escape my chest, cold sweat stuck to the nape of my neck. Oblivious to the chill, I ran to the other side of the house and pulled open the front door. It was the only other way out. The only logical, practical way out. Banked snow five feet deep blocked my way. Luckily it didn't fall into the hallway, in my heart I knew she hadn't gone out that way. It didn't seem real or possible. There was no other way out. She had to be in the house somewhere so I ran through all the rooms again, checking for her. It was ridiculous.

Where had she gone? Why would she go?

I found myself back in the kitchen where Andy was still standing at the door, although he'd had the good sense to close it behind him. He had one hand nervously on the latch as if he was contemplating getting out easily. He looked at me like I was a lunatic, his eyebrows raised, eyes narrowed, mouth tense, which to be honest I wasn't really surprised about.

"A woman was here already. … we had tea…I'm not sure what's happened"

The look on his face showed that not only he didn't believe me, but that he was leaving as soon as he could in case I was dangerous.

I rubbed my head in my hands and struggled to control my breathing, I felt my heart bump around in my chest. All the time I knew he was watching me silently, intently. My mouth and throat were so dry that my voice croaked and I struggled to speak. Yet I knew I had to regain control if there would be any chance of him listening to me, and I so wanted to change the expression on his face.

"Please believe me. A woman was here. She said she knew Gran. We were looking at Gran's journals." As I spoke I ran over to the press to check that the journals were really gone. Because if they were still there, although I didn't want to believe it, that would mean that I had made up the whole morning. The woman, the chat, the tea, everything would have been imagined. Fear gripped me then. My heart bounced painfully in my chest, I couldn't swallow, adrenalin had dried my throat. I saw my hands were shaking as I reached to open the cupboard door, mentally noting if that was a sign of madness and wondering if Andy had noticed. With some concern for my sanity, I scanned the wide wooden shelves. Everything was in its usual perfect order, bottles labelled, and the smell of lavender filled the air. The space where the journals always sat was empty. My hand tightened, clutching the door to stop me fall. I needed its strength in that moment. Andy moved closer to me, and patted my shoulder with a large gloved hand.

"Grief and sadness can play with your mind, you know? There's no shame in it. Kirsten has been helping me get over the death of my parents. She was always so kind. And I was hoping for some help with this flu thing, so I could feel better. Because sometimes when you don't physically feel alright it can mess with your head as well."

I shook my head at him. Staring at him straight in the eye, I could see in his face that he didn't believe me, and I didn't blame him. It seemed crazy.

"Look I used the tractor to get over from the other valley. I've cleared your road and path. The snow was eight feet deep in places. No one could have walked through it. There is nothing moving on the roads, some of the drifts are twenty feet high. Seriously, nothing is moving out there. And I'll tell you another thing, there were no footsteps at your door. I don't see how anyone could have walked through. You would have needed a snow shovel to dig your way through."

I shivered then. A chill spreading through my bones. I'd been here before. Feeling the same way. Strange things happening to me, and unable to explain them. Was it happening again? When would my life be back to normal? A whisper came into my mind. *This is your normal.* I gulped back my panic, that horrible pain that could come into my stomach so easily. All the warning signs were there this morning, and I had ignored them. Where would this latest event lead? I shivered again, aware of a darkening of the skies outside.

"She said she had come through from Glasgow by train". Even as the words left my brain and escaped my mouth I knew that wasn't true. She hadn't answered me when I'd asked. There was no explanation for the strange event. Or at least not one I could talk to this guy about. I needed to talk to Angel and Grizelle. They would understand and they would help. If they could. I grasped in my pocket, "look, she wrote down the name of a petrol station for me. This proves she was here." I pulled out an old dried-up leaf, it broke up into dust in my hand. My pockets were empty of anything else. Andy's eyebrows shot up.

"Trains are all off, snow on the line and frozen points. This is the worst snow Lanarkshire has had in years. I'm not sure what you think has happened, but there is no way anyone could have got here." He slowed his words as he spoke, like he was talking to a child or someone insane. I could see his mouth moving in exaggeration as if he did so I would understand easier. I could tell that he thought I was unstable or worse.

"Well someone or something was here, and they've taken Gran's books. Look …"I gestured towards the bare shelves with my hands, "where are they then?"

"I'm really sorry for your loss." He said as his huge frame backed towards the door, his feet light for such a big man. Emotion flickered over his face, he gulped, his eyes not meeting mine

"…..as I said, grief can make us do strange things, and you have been here on your own for a while. Maybe you are dehydrated or something. Are you on medication…?" His voice trailed off as if he could sense I was about to kill him.

It was no use. He really thought I was imagining it all. I had to get out and see Angel and Grizelle.

"Can I call you a doctor?"

That was the last straw. "I don't need a doctor, thanks." Each syllable spat out in frustration.

"I'm sorry I can't help with your *man* flu." I had to make that point, childish I know, but how dare he suggest that I was ill or insane.

"You'll be wanting to get home now. Maybe you should visit the doctor yourself for that *wee* cold." I dismissed him by holding the door open which I immediately regretted. The chill was unbelievable, standing there without a coat, hat or gloves.

As he squeezed past me, I sensed a great sadness, in fact I was overcome and could feel a pain in my heart. I knew Gran had indeed helped him. Trying to see it from his point of view, I knew I couldn't let it go like this.

"Thanks for clearing the snow. That was really kind of you. I know I can't convince you, but there was someone here, and they have stolen Gran's journals. I appreciate it must look a bit mad. It feels like that to me as well. I don't understand it, I need to find out what's happened."

"Let me take you into the town" he offered. Striding ahead pulling on his hat.

"I don't want to leave you here in the cottage alone. Maybe you'll feel better with people around you."

There was no point in arguing with him. And if this had happened to someone I knew a couple of weeks ago, I would probably have behaved the same way. Except that given my recent experiences I knew there could be always be another explanation. One that might take me to a place I thought I'd never have to revisit.

I was practical even if my mind was somewhere else, and I grabbed my things, pulling on my coat and stumbled along jumping into his footsteps in the deep snow as I followed him to where the tractor sat outside the garden wall.

He was right, as I suppose I knew he would be. There was only one set of foot prints, huge holes in the snow from his feet, and I could see where he'd dragged the snow back to make his walk easier. However, that woman as I was now calling her, however she had got to the cottage, she hadn't walked along that path, and yet I had seen her standing at my door, thigh high in snow. It didn't make sense. I turned away from my little white cottage, already fading into a storm of sleet, pulling my scarf around me, and I trudged along in Andy's steps.

The landscape was beautiful like an artist had painted a typical Christmas card scene. The hills and mountains in the distance blurred against the cloud line. Sleet was falling and although Andy said he'd cleared the road, it was disappearing quickly under a new covering of fresh snow. Pulling my coat around me, hat, scarf and gloves on, despite their protection I was still chilled to the bone within minutes. Andy helped me up into the frozen cabin, the stench of diesel made me feel sick, and I tried not to sit too close to him on the tight little bench seat. Perched so high up in the tractor I felt every movement and sway as in silence we bumped across the road, and cut across the fields as a short cut into town. As we rode along I became increasingly oblivious to the snow scene. Inside I was close to tears. Even though it looked mad, I knew someone or something had visited me that morning. And they had taken Gran's precious journals. I had no idea why they wanted them. And I didn't know how I could get them back, yet I knew I had to try. Shame and sadness flooded through me. I was taken in by her sympathy and that she said she knew Gran. I knew nothing else about her, and yet I'd gallantly opened up Gran's cupboard, even though I knew she'd never do that.

What was I thinking? How could I have been so stupid?

Andy didn't attempt to make conversation on the trip, and hurriedly dropped me off with a quick wave outside St Mary's, the huge gothic style cathedral across from the graveyard where we'd buried Gran. It was also the place I'd had all the recent strange experiences. I couldn't help it, as soon as that thought came into my mind other angry self-pitying thoughts followed. Perhaps I was mad, and had imagined everything. Perhaps I had more in common with my mother than I'd ever realised, after all she had ended up in an institution. A spiral of loathing dragged me down into darkness and hot tears stung my eyes as I slipped along the icy covered cobbled street.

This was one of the oldest parts of town, and the grave-yard and Church sat high above the town as sentinel. My family had such an important role in safeguarding the peace of the place. I'd had no idea of the sacrifice required, and Gran had offered the ultimate sacrifice to ensure that her neighbours and their children and grandchildren could live in safety. I didn't feel I was that brave and I suppose the responsibility of being the last in the line was bound to feel heavy on me. I'd thought my part in all of that was over, so I was worried about what the morning's event might mean. My feet took me along the familiar road, snow falling again all around me. The road was empty of traffic or pedestrians, and the street lights were on in an attempt to cut through the gloom. I was frozen faced in the wind chill, but my eyes burned by the time I got to the glass fronted stone building that was *Angel's Cakes*. Nestled against the side wall of the Church it offered fabulous food and lots of angel products like pictures, wall hangings and music. Ever since I discovered it I'd always felt calm and peaceful inside listening to beautiful music and eating cakes. I'd met Gran's friends here as well, Angel and Grizelle and both had supported me physically, emotionally and most importantly spiritually as I'd investigated Gran's untimely death. It was the most obvious place for me to head to, and I was looking forward to seeing the two of them.

Disappointment hit me as I saw it was in darkness with a *sorry we are closed* sign on the glass door. Sniffing back tears, I wiped my face with gloved hands. This close to all the potential angelic assistance though something changed in my mood. Maybe it was my imagination, or my madness, I could feel whispers of support, like someone had stepped behind me and was holding me up. I closed my eyes for a moment and sensed Gran coming closer, just like my dream that morning. She was there. I wasn't alone and she wanted me to know that.

At that moment, the mobile phone in my pocket whistled as a number of text and voicemail messages came through. Back in town I had a better signal than at the cottage. Taking the phone from my pocket there were six voice messages from friends in London, checking up on me, calling to say hello, wanting to let me know they were thinking of me. I instantly felt better on hearing their voices. There was a message from Angel, followed with a text to let me know that the café was closed due to the weather, and that she was inside with Grizelle, and I was to knock loudly or call when I arrived.

A smile touched my lips, and realised that I'd moved from sadness to happiness in moments. A testimony to the power of friendship and great timing for me, and I also realised, I had to remember this, that even in the darkest of times, everything could change instantly. Nothing lasted for ever.

With that thought, I turned and tapped on the glass and in the darkness of the café, a light appeared and within a few minutes my friend Angel, all smiles, laughing, she noisily dragged me into a long hug, full of love and appreciation. She had been such a support to me, and I wanted to hear her news.

Chapter Five

Angel looked different. She was always brightly dressed, that was the first thing I'd noticed, I could see that she had a new glow about her.

"Have you had your hair done?" I asked. "There's something different about you."

She threw her head back in a gesture I loved, and laughed loudly at that, and pointed over to the back of the room where Grizelle had risen from one of the wooden pews Angel used as seating in her café. Grizelle had been a school mate of my gran's, and was easily in her mid 70s, but what a powerhouse of a woman. She ran her own antiques business, which involved lots of travel to fairs, auctions and house-clearances, and she always looked smart and stylish. Always in tweed, muted colours of the landscape, heathers, greens and browns. She too had a different look. She was glowing too.

Grizelle embraced me, holding me in a long special hug, and whispered in my ear. "Your gran is fine Kirsty, I was dreaming of her this morning. She loves you so much. Don't forget that."

Grizelle and Gran had a very special relationship reaching back seventy years, with all the life changes that can bring, birth, marriage, deaths, hope, excitement, sadness, grief. They also had a strong psychic connection, and here she was telling me exactly what I needed to hear. I breathed in her musky scent. Even though I'd known these two women only a short time, their strength, compassion and love for me and my grandmother had kept me going over the last few weeks. I couldn't imagine now my world without them.

As we sat across the table from each other, Angel brought over a fresh pot of tea, and an empty mug adorned with angels for me. She disappeared again behind the counter, before coming back over with a huge plate of scones and cakes, and gestured for us to help ourselves. In her other hand she carried a large piece of white quartz crystal. It was unpolished so looked like a chunk of ice, as if she had plucked it from the ground outside.

I was used to her crystal loving ways, and trusted her absolutely to introduce a piece completely appropriate to help my mood. Unbidden she explained as she always did.

"White quartz to bring balance and clarity to our thoughts, I had a feeling we might need it today."

"I don't know where to begin….." I started, suddenly embarrassed to explain what had happened.

"There is no hurry Kirsty." said Grizelle in her deep, cultured voice "You take your time."

"Thank you Grizelle, mmmmm! Angel these are delicious!" For a moment I was lost in the texture and taste on my tongue from Angel's home-made scones, butter and raspberry jam. Hot out of the oven, and I could see a freshly iced carrot cake waiting for me. Her café was the best in a town renowned for its cakes. Every coffee shop and café competed each year for the coveted 'Best Baker' title. Angel had won it for the last two years. She had created a little spiritual spa in this ancient town, in an old stone building beside the church. Inside, candles sat on each table, with candelabra overhead, exposed stone walls old wooden tables and church pews, and at the side of the café was a small shop area selling every type of angel product you could imagine. There was a sense of calm here, and at the front of the café area she had put up a conservatory so it was great for people watching. I was addicted to her cakes and the savoury comfort food she and her small team provided. She believed in the power of crystals and angels and her love for them was apparent in everything she did. At first I'd thought she was slightly mad, until I realised that everything she did was about love, and it made me reflect on how much I didn't recognise that in my own life. I wondered if I resisted it. I had learned so much from her and Grizelle in a very short time.

Looking at her today in the semi darkness at the back of the café, I noted again that she looked different. Her bright blue eyes behind purple rimmed glasses sparked like her crystals. She looked like a child with a secret bursting to tell all.

"Before I tell you what happened to me today" I said in between sips of tea and nibbles of cake.

"Can I ask, Angel what's different with you? You look so happy."

She blushed slightly and looked away and back to me like a young girl would. I had a sense of what she would say. She was always talking about angels and her love for them, yet this looked to me like old fashioned romance. I'd always been able to spot it in friends.

"Have you met someone?" I meant someone special though I didn't need to say it. She looked in love.

She burst out laughing again "Yes!" she shouted. And we had to laugh along with her.

"Tell all" I said, filling up the cups. We leaned in towards each other conspiratorially, even though the place was empty and locked against the snow storm still raging outside. The smell of incense reached me, sandalwood filled me up and I felt my breathing deepen and that in turn relaxed me. Muscle by muscle I could feel the magic of the place soothe my soul, and laughter and friendship all combining into a salve for my spirit and body. I was so happy to hear their news.

"Before I tell you anything, I meant to ask, do you want to stay upstairs in the flat at least tonight? The stove is warm, the heating is on, there's lots of food and you'd be very welcome. The cottage must be freezing and the roads are still difficult to get through, what do you say?"

What else could I say? The old me would have played the martyr, insisting that the cottage was fine, that I could manage. Angel had always shown me such support and hospitality, and I had stayed with her after Gran's funeral, so instead I nodded my head in gratitude. Her flat was gorgeous, comfortable and warm, with a beautiful view of the floodlit church. It was a haven. She waved away my thanks, still sitting beaming at the world, like a very satisfied being. Grizelle sat back a little, giving Angel her place to continue, settling against some cushions, even though she probably knew the story already. I adopted the same stance, feeling so peaceful and calm, whether from the warm café ambiance, the company of friends, the power of the quartz, or the angels all around us I didn't know or care. I was happy and contented and the morning's events felt like a million miles away.

"It's Malcom" she said calmly looking at me, and then took a bite of scone, chewing it thoroughly whilst I waited for more.

"Malcolm? Your ex-husband Malcolm?" I asked just to clarify even though of course I knew this.

"We met, we talked, we still love each other, we're back together again"

I was shocked and as she looked at my expression she laughed again.

"Don't look like that! You'll never guess where we met up?"

I did not have a clue, and must have shrugged. After all when I first met Angel she seemed so certain and sure that she had no feelings for her ex-husband Malcolm, and I thought he had met someone else. She had seemed so happy with her single life, and perhaps that was the best time to meet someone.

She was laughing so much I could hardly make out what she said

"In a yoga class" she squealed "we met in a yoga class."

With that Grizelle joined in the laughter as well, and I remembered. When I first met Angel she told me that she had met her Guardian Angel at a yoga class. I had been fascinated with the story, and then my gran had helped her to reconnect with her angels, her life changed and Angel's Cakes was born.

"A *yoga* class! What happened to him? I thought he wasn't into anything like that?"

"I know, it seems unlikely, but it's obvious that our soul journey together in this life time isn't over."

Angel never failed to surprise me. Only she could explain reuniting with her ex in that way.

"Tell me everything. You look different, younger, and happier, if that's even possible. I don't know what to think, how did he end up at a yoga class?"

"I took it as a sign" she said laughing again, "I bumped into him coming out of the Body and Spirit Centre, standing there with his yoga mat under his arm. I really saw him properly for the first time in years. Like he was when we were young and first together. He was laughing with some other people, and he looked happy and carefree. He was so pleased to see me and asked if we could talk. He said he had hoped to meet me, and that since the divorce he said he hadn't stopped thinking of us, and he felt guilty that he had given up so quickly. He was in a bad place feeling that he couldn't support me after the death of my parents. And when he said that I realised how much I had shut him out at that time. My grief and maybe my rage at the unfairness of it all meant I was blaming everyone else for what is a natural thing. Life and death, it happens to us all, and I was in a place of being a victim with grief and living a life that didn't fulfil me, and rather taking control of that, I was trying to control the stuff that can't be controlled. Like I was scared to make decisions in my own life in case I got it wrong or failed in some way. Anyway we really talked, so honestly and I felt connected. More importantly I suppose, we really listened to each other. We were polite at first, like the way strangers are, but it was in a good way, showing each other respect."

Angel stopped for a moment, and wiped a tear from the corner of her eye, before she continued.

"Malcolm said that he was angry at the time...really angry with me that I had changed my life, that he saw me taking control and it made him feel more of a victim. He felt that he couldn't talk about it and instead it was easier just to walk away. Strangely it was as he saw me making a success of my new life, my angels, my workshops, my flat and my wee business inspired him to make changes as well. Can you believe he retrained as a reflexologist? He was offering free treatments to a local carers centre and one of his new colleagues took him to yoga. He said he loved it and felt a connection with all that I'd done. That got him thinking about me, us and all that we'd had together. It's funny, Malcolm and I started off as friends, long before our romance started, and that's what he offered to me that night after meeting again, within a few days the old feelings flooded back. I was so shocked and surprised, and even though I was already happy, it was as if angels and the universe decided that romantic love was there for me as well. Even at my age."

I was enthralled, her love for him shone from her, and I realised that I would love to find that too. I hadn't had it with my ex, and I sent a prayer to heaven, please let me experience that love before I die. Please let me feel that way and meet someone who can make me shine, like I want them to shine too. Tears filled my eyes, I hadn't realised I wanted it so much.

"So we are making up for last time," she let out a loud, dirty laugh "And I've more or less moved into his house, so my flat is free Kirsty, for as long as you need it. Now please tell us what's happened. You looked like you'd seen a ghost when you came in…"

"Maybe I did" I said, voicing the little worry that had been in my mind since this morning. "Maybe I did."

I took a deep breath and told them the story, from the strange woman arriving at the door, the tea, the chat, smelly

Andy arriving, which I knew was cruel but I couldn't help it, the books, the mysterious disappearance, the snow, the lack of footprints. I omitted the loneliness, guilt, shame, fear for my sanity and all the negative self-talk I'd indulged in on my way into town. Instead I'd pulled a face and shrugged that I felt bad about it. Angel hugged me, and Grizelle rubbed my hand. They knew what I meant and didn't need to say anything. It just helped to tell them all about it.

"Signs" Grizelle said. "I was dreaming of your gran this morning and she left me with a message, "to watch out for sign". This is it girls, something is happening again."

"I had the same words in my dream this morning" I added.

"Me too" said Angel. We all looked at each other. The other two, my brave friends both put a protective arm around me.

"Kirsty, you've not to worry about this. You can deal with anything that comes your way, remember that. You are never on your own. You know that." Angel said.

And although I knew there was some truth in what she said, fear gripped my heart in a chilled spiked glove, and I gulped. They hadn't gone where I'd gone, they hadn't had to face what I'd faced. With their support I felt better, good perhaps, but not invincible. A little shadow of apprehension sat in my mind, a reminder.

You have madness in your family. You can't cope.

I smiled at them and nodded my head although I don't think I convinced either them or me. I felt scared again. Angel sensed it as always and moved the quartz closer to me, then pushed it into my hand.

"Hold this and breathe deep" she said "close your eyes for a moment let the crystal help, ask for support. Then let it happen, go with whatever comes into your mind."

For a moment I did that, closing my eyes, breathing deep, and my mind filled with a white fog, lightness and then I heard a heartbeat. Deep, low and strong. My eyes flicked open.

"I heard something!" I said. As I looked at them I knew they'd sensed it to. "What does it mean Grizelle?"

"A sign" is all she said, she breathed deeply and whispered,

"Of the living heart perhaps. Mother Earth. Whatever you have to do, it's something to do with the earth. We need to watch out for signs, they will unfold in time. You need to go with the guidance that comes into your mind Kirsty, and follow that. I feel that the beating heart will guide you."

It's times like that when I felt completely lost. Grizelle was a very intelligent woman, and very connected spiritually and psychically but I was a novice at all of that. I though back to all the times Gran had tried to show me what she did as she created her lotions and potions. All the times she wanted to include me in what she created and the knowledge she had, and all the times I ignored her and excused myself. I hadn't wanted to know and now that it was too late, regret sat like a hard rock in my heart, I felt its heaviness.

"Kirsty what do you feel you have to do now? Have you had dreams of where you need to go?" Angel asked, still sitting with her arm close to me, I was immediately comforted and supported. The weight lifted for a moment. I could breathe again.

"I was dreaming of Newgrange. I've had a horrible feeling about it since my Dad called and asked me for help. It's the first I've heard his voice in years, and yet I don't know what to do. Should I go to Ireland and see him?" I looked from one face to the other, searching for an answer I knew could only come from inside of me.

"A part of me would love to, especially now Gran has gone, but there's a bit of me so angry that he left me and hasn't been in touch for years. I mean, I actually had thought he had died. That's what I've said for years." My voice shook, I swallowed and felt a sadness overcome me, a black cage to separate me from those who cared.

What kind of father could he be when he left me like that, abandoned me, rejected me? And what kind of daughter was I to think so?

Tears filled Angel's eyes as she looked at me with compassion and understanding.

"Don't be too hard on yourself, it's a tough time dealing with grief and shock. I always say to people be kind to yourself following any trauma. And keep being kind to yourself. It can take a couple of years to cope with the passing of a loved one, even when you can have a close spiritual or psychic connection, you are still having to adapt to the lack of their physical presence. So don't rush into any kind of recrimination. We all do what we can, we make decisions based on what we know at the time. All we have to remember is that we are loved. I might sound like an old hippy at times, but it's taken me years to realise that life is simple. We live, we love, we die. For some reason we forget that and try to overcomplicate things. It's our thoughts that mess things up, we can always choose our thoughts."

She had said this to me before that our thoughts are in their nature random, we put the meaning to particular ones, usually the negative thoughts, and then tell ourselves stories about those thoughts. Making things up and stressing and worrying about stuff is a story, neither true nor likely to occur. So we permit our thoughts to torment us.

Her wise words made me smile. She was right, I was worrying about something I knew nothing about. Until I spoke to my father or heard from him I really didn't know his story. I was using words like abandonment and rejection when I didn't know anything, other than they made me feel bad.

Why would I want to feel bad about myself? I didn't know that yet. All I knew was I had a habit of negative feelings brought on by judging myself. I wanted to stop this.

"So how do I stop it Angel? How do I stop thinking negatively?"

She nodded at Grizelle, who smiled and said,

"Kirsty you don't, actually you can't stop thinking. Thoughts are random. They have no negative or positive charge. They are only thoughts. If you don't focus on one, another will pop into your mind immediately. I think Buddhists call it the monkey mind. Meditation helps me. I suppose it's the way our brains work. We don't have to contemplate that. All we need to know is that thought is there, it just is. It's the way we deal with thought that makes a difference to our lives, and that's the only part of this we can control. When a thought comes into your mind, you can either give it your attention or not, that is up to you. If you appreciate that it's just a random thought, then it can come and go. The only question you have to consider is do you want to feel happy or sad? Calm or angry? It's not the thought that changes our state of emotion. Our emotions are there already, we attach the emotion to the thought. So if you are angry in some way, you feel that all your thoughts are angry. They are not, they are neutral, completely state less. You focus unconsciously on the angry ones, and the others you let go. If you can remember that you instantly return to a balanced state. Do you understand?"

"I think I do, so it's like I am making an unconscious choice to choose thoughts that mirror my sadness inside? And then I think that's my reality all around me? And I suppose that's why my mood can change so quickly?"

She nodded, answering what would have been my next question for me

"All you can do is monitor your thoughts, see them for all that they are, random firings of neurons in your brain, and appreciate that we can think. That's a magnificent thing. Remember though that you don't have to be trapped in that emotion. Recognise and own your emotions, be aware of the emotional state you are in, and then don't let yourself follow thoughts into a dark place. You don't need to do that."

We sat in companionable silence for a short time, Grizelle's words going around in my mind. Angel popped on some music. Low rhythmic drum beats and a women chanting "aum" over and over. The sound of the universe Angel had said before. Warmth, the sound, the smells of incense and food and drink, the atmosphere of companionship. All felt good and I relaxed into the cushions some more. Angel refilled the teapot, and appeared again with hot vegetable soup and some Irish soda bread she had baked this morning. She grinned when I raised an eyebrow at her.

"Where next for you?" she asked and I had to return her smile.

Newgrange was in my dreams, a Stone Age temple somewhere in Ireland. That's where I was going, and hopefully I could meet my dad and find out his story. First though, another place came into my mind. The Druid's Temple in Glasgow. Something was nudging me towards it. That woman at the house this morning, perhaps I'd find out something about her and Gran's books. Follow one sign at a time, that's all I had to do. I wanted to visit there first.

"Despite what you think, I feel I need to try and find the Druid's Temple before I got to Ireland. Do either of you want to come with me?" I would have really appreciated their insight and knowledge as I had no idea really about any of it.

Both nodded enthusiastically, except they couldn't get away over the next few days. Angel said she thought the trains could be back on the next day, that her car was in for a service otherwise I could have borrowed that. Grizelle said she was taking some time off and heading to the Orkney Isles for a while.

There was something about that which caught my attention and I had to ask. "Grizelle, the Orkneys? At this time of year?"

I thought it had to be for an antiques' auction, I mean what other reason could there be to visit the Orkney Islands sitting over ten miles off the coast of Northern Scotland in December? It would be freezing.

"What are you planning to do there? Is it for your business?" Even as I said it I knew there was something else. Something important.

"There is some work we need to do."

"Are you flying? It's such a long way. I'd love to go and visit the ancient sites. What is it called again?"

"Skara Brae." As she said it I felt a shiver, a faint tremor in my body.

I missed her use of the "we" word at the time, focused as I was on her travel arrangements and reason for going.

"I have a feeling flights might be difficult." She looked around her and readjusted her heather coloured tweed shawl close around her shoulders before continuing. "We'll be on a boat."

"A cruise?" I squealed. "How lovely....but a bit cold at this time of year!"

"Not a cruise...... as such." She seemed guarded, almost reluctant to say much. She wasn't giving anything away, again she pulled her shawl around her, and seemed to hesitate before she spoke. Her fingers fluffing up her short grey hair.

"It is all quite confidential, and I wish I could say more. However, I have promised not to divulge too much. Suffice to say I have decided to take some time off to satisfy an idea I have. Something I wish I'd done years ago."

Seeming to make up her mind she leaned close, her older wrinkled hand covering mine. I traced the age spots in my mind, so like Gran's it was strangely comforting. Her face softened, and she whispered

"I think you do have to note this Kirsty, for the work you will be doing in Ireland." She looked straight in my eyes, her hand grasped mine tightly. Dark shadows moved closer to us as if they too wanted to know more.

"I need to be there, in the Isles. It's a promise I made to a dear friend many years ago, and I really cannot say more about that. The opportunity has now arisen for me to join an environmental activist boat to try to save the whales near the Orkneys. So for me it's perfect timing. Its important work, and needs to be done. I can't ignore it any longer. I need to help." She pursed her lips and sipped her tea, sitting back a little whilst she waited for my reaction.

Angel and Grizelle burst out laughing at my expression. I knew it was one of shock, puzzlement and was one I wore often in their company. Grizelle was very passionate about the earth and I knew she was involved with Granny with crystals and stuff like that, *but to live on a boat off the North of Scotland in the middle of winter?* It was madness. She was well into her seventies.

How on earth would she survive that? As the surprise lessened I had to admit to myself she was fit and hearty, and if anything like my grandmother, the cold probably wouldn't affect her at all. These older women were strong, sturdy and determined. It's what had got them through life in harder times.

So why was I so surprised? From what she had told me before, she had beaten alcoholism, created a successful business after financial ruin, and survived a very unhappy marriage. *Why should age stop her doing what she always wanted?* What would I have said to Gran if she had come up with the same suggestion? Actually it was the sort of thing Gran would have done if she could.

I smiled, nodding my head

"Brilliant Grizelle, good for you. Please tell me you'll be wearing thermal undies," and with that we all laughed loudly. "You might also get to see the Northern Lights. Now, that would be amazing. I'd love to see them."

"Well perhaps you will Kirsty, you never know." Smiled Grizelle. "But I don't think many others will." I wasn't sure what she meant, and before I could ask, Angel refilled all the tea cups, and offered more cake. My stomach groaned in fullness, it was more than I'd had to eat for days, and too delicious that I couldn't say no.

When we had all finally stopped nibbling and as Angel cleared some of the plates away, wiping up crumbs from the solid wooden table, a tiny little pure white feather lay in the middle of the table. Angel immediately sat back down, arms full of crockery.

"It's a sign" she gasped. "Thank you Angels!" She beamed at us. "It's a sign." She said again, quieter this time.

"But of what?" I asked.

"We'll soon find out if there's more, "said Grizelle. "Personally I like to think it's to let us know that angels are with us, all the time."

We all sat in silence for a few seconds, Angel leaned over the table suddenly serious.

"I need to give you something." She scribbled a symbol on the back of a napkin.

"It's important that you use this when you connect with Archangel Michael. Remember he will protect you always."

A little shiver ran down my spine, and I was aware of the silent space we sat in, despite the howling wind and snow hitting off the glass conservatory. The lights shimmered a little.

"This is the ancient symbol of Archangel Michael. When you see it you will know that he is there. Use your intuition as your guide. Don't forget."

She pushed the napkin into my pocket, rubbing her hand over my head as if in a blessing. She headed back into the kitchen with a smile. I was surprised and took her departure as an opportunity to ask Grizelle more about what she had said about the whales.

"Kirsty, whales are dying all over the Atlantic coastline. Apparently healthy animals, whole groups of whales are beaching all around the coast of the British Isles. Haven't you seen that on the television?"

I nodded, I had, yet not really taken too much notice.

"So…. what can you do about it?" I asked and as I did so I felt a little shiver trying to draw my attention to something. The way it had happened earlier.

"What do you really think is happening?" I asked. We instinctively moved closer together. Some lights from a passing car lit up our table for a moment and I could see the emotion flick fast across her face. Her lines deepening as she considered what to tell me.

"We believe that the US military are using a new sound wave technology and it has had a negative impact on whales, disrupting their sonar systems, so basically how they navigate around the seas. And this is distressing them so much that they are beaching in places they don't know and would never have visited before. It's terrible. It's hurting me Kirsty. I can't explain why, it just does. I feel that it's time for me to get more involved. All this information used to be hard to find, now with the internet we can all share and keep each other informed."

There was a loud bang against the glass door behind us, and we all jumped in fright. Angel facing the door, quickly recovered her composure and headed over to open it. Grizelle spoke quickly to me.

"Look it up online Kirsty, it's terrible, but I feel at my age I can contribute and try my best to do something about it. Or perhaps I might die trying."

It was only a phrase, one that was used every day, again that little chill visited me briefly, touching me sharply on the back of my shoulders with an iced hand, and I shivered, one word was whispered in my inner ear. "Signs."

What could I say? She had always been a sensible woman, she had every right to go and do what she wanted. I wished her well with a hug of support. I hoped that when I was that age I could follow a passion. Another faint whisper in my inner ear, *"If you reach that age"*. I shivered again.

Chapter Six

ngel opened the door and the sound of her loud laugh reached us as paper napkins flew about in the blast of wind which whipped around the table. What looked like a living snowman burst in to the café, also laughing and joking. She introduced us to Malcolm, and once he had shaken off some of the snow which fell from his coat melting as it hit the floor, he shook hands formally with me. Grizelle had known him for years, and there was affection in their grins and good natured banter. He had a kind face, from what I could see as he kept on his hat and coat. He apologised for the snow which was dropping from his body as he moved further into the room, and explained that he wanted to walk Angel home. The roads were still not cleared and potentially dangerous, and he counselled Grizelle not to take her car out that night.

He was lovely, pink cheeked from the icy winds he'd battled to get to the cafe, and with his brightly coloured scarf he matched Angel's multi coloured garments perfectly. I had an immediate good feeling about him, and to think they had let this relationship go. It was lovely to see. For only a brief moment I wondered if it would be possible to reunite with Derek in London, yet as soon as I said it, I knew deep inside that it wouldn't work. The feelings just weren't there anymore. I wanted more than he could offer. As lonely as I felt at times, I didn't want to make do anymore.

We took his entrance as time to leave, and I helped Angel into the kitchen with the cups and things we'd used. She filled some bags and tubs with the leftover food, and slipped them into my hands along with the keys for the flat upstairs. It would be a relief to spend a night there. It had such a lovely atmosphere and would be warm.

As we hugged and said our farewells quickly outside, the chill hit us all. Someone called to Grizelle from across the street, and I waited with her for the few minutes it took for a woman in a heavy coat to trudge over the snow covered road. Caught in the yellow street lighting at this old part of town, she looked like she'd stepped from a Victorian melodrama as the wind caught the end of her long white hair, tossing it behind her like a cloak. I realised that it was one of the Faslane peace camp environmentalists we'd all met a few weeks ago. Her lined face showed the years more than her walk, posture or clothes did, and she hugged Grizelle tightly. They both laughed and turned arm in arm, helping each other as they picked their way tentatively along the pavements towards Grizelle's flat. She still lived above her antiques shop which sat at the top of the High Street. A shop stuffed with every kind of collectable you could imagine. And one that always scared me in case I accidentally broke something. It wasn't designed for browsing. Angel and Malcolm trudged along behind them, laughing and singing a Christmas carol. I heard their rendition of Good King Wenceslas fading away into the night. It was a funny sight, and again I felt I had missed something as I turned towards the alley beside the coffee shop. The festive song made me feel sad for a moment, a little melancholy for what I'd never had.

The snow was falling heavily again and night had drawn in, as my gran used to say. In this part of Scotland it was dark by early afternoon, and the street lamps' glow faded under the heavy snow skies. The road was quiet, very little traffic able to get through and no footsteps had added to mine from earlier in the day. With another shiver I walked as quickly as the underfoot conditions allowed along the alley between the café and the church wall on my way to Angel's flat. I was pensive as I walked past the hidden doorway I knew sat in the shadow of the wall. I never wanted to open that door again, it seemed like another lifetime ago.

The morning's events came back into mind, I had really thought my life would be uncomplicated and that I had faced all my demons. A feeling of dread in the pit of my stomach seemed to suggest otherwise, and I tried to shrug it off and hurried along. My breath steamed in the air around me, and I pulled my scarf closely around my neck. It was colder than I'd ever known it.

Within a few minutes after only a couple of slips in the deep snow, I crunched my way into the yard behind the café and carefully climbed up the stone steps to the flat. The noise of my slow steps muffled by the snow. I unlocked the door, flicked on the lights, and blinked as my eyes adjusted to the brightness. I moved quickly into the lounge and the glass fronted stove, filling it with logs, kindling and firelighters. It immediately came to life and within minutes roared heat and light into the room, with the smell of pitchy pine.

I loved this home. The heating had clicked on and I popped my goodies into the kitchen, flicking on the kettle. Angel had said to help myself to her toiletries and I had left a toothbrush and some clothes from when I'd stayed there before, so I had everything I needed. I ran a bath and spent some time lying back in the bubbles, I hadn't been able to do that at Grans as in the last week it had been too cold to spend time in the bathroom. I felt relaxation soaking into my bones as the heat worked its magic. I wish I'd put on some music or the t.v. before I'd jumped in. The complete quiet was unnerving, and eventually I couldn't stand it. Rather than fully relaxing I was thinking back to this morning. That woman had completely taken me in, and I was angry at her and even more so, angry at myself for trusting her.

How could I have been so stupid? And to let those precious journals out of my sight.

I decided to get to Temple in Glasgow as soon as I could. Perhaps the petrol station she mentioned might know her after all she was really distinctive. So tiny, with all that long dark hair, *like a little pixie* I thought, and then I shivered again, in spite of the heat.

I dried quickly and pulled on some red tartan pyjamas, pink fleece dressing gown from the back of the bedroom door, and a pair of white and pink bunny faced slippers Angel kept and we had laughed about last time I was here. I put my clothes in the washer dryer so they'd be ready in the morning, warmed some soup, buttered soda bread and returned to the sofa and the comfort from the stove. I probably ate far too fast, as her food was always delicious. I turned on the television and found an old comedy movie to watch. Anything to take my mind off the loss of the journals.

Last time I'd stayed it was only a few days after Gran's death, and I had been plagued with nightmares as the horror of what had happened had slowly unravelled. It was so weird that I was there again and I really hoped that I could sleep soundly. I suppose I was putting off bedtime as long as I could. Living on my own didn't seem to be good for me, and rather than feeling independent and free, I was brooding and lonely. It might be better after I'd decorated the cottage and had some of my own things around me. My friends Jen and Suzy had driven up with a van full my possessions last weekend, before the weather had changed. It had been fabulous to see them, and they'd loved the cottage and the town. I hadn't had the energy or inclination to unpack anything. All the boxes sat broodingly in the corner of the kitchen for now taunting me with their presence. Lazy and a failure they silently said.

I wiped away sad tears. Too much time to think, that was my problem right then. I needed to find some work, something to occupy my mind for a while. I'd ask Angel if I could help out in the café, or find some bar work at one of the town pubs, until I could decide what to do.

By the side of the stove, Angel had stacked a pile of books. I glanced over and noticed that at the top was a book about Ireland. I quickly flicked through and found some pages devoted to the Boyne valley and the town of Drogheda. It looked beautiful, picturesque and with substantial buildings. I was too tired to read it properly. As I closed it I noticed a photograph of a site with a large stone mound surrounded by smaller ones, topped with grass roofs. It said it was a place called Knowth, near Newgrange. I had a pang of something in my heart. A familiarity, a longing. I wasn't sure what it was.

I took the book into the bedroom with me. I remembered about the napkin Angel had written on, and pulled it out of my pocket to have a better look.

What was it she'd said? A symbol of Archangel Michael?

On the paper were some lines, as if someone had tried to join up some dots, like you saw with a star constellation. It didn't make any sense to me, so I left it by the bed. As sleep took me, my last thoughts were that I'd go to Ireland soon. With Christmas coming up I realised I wanted to find my Dad. I didn't want a festive season on my own.

Angel's flat worked its magic and I slept deeply all night. Waking up at eight still in darkness, I could hear water running. A sudden unexpected thaw, sleet rather than snow, grey sky and slush on the pavements. Drips from the drain pipes outside the bedroom window. I was relieved, the trains would be on again and I could head into Glasgow to find Jane and the journals she'd stolen from me. I could feel my mood lighten with purpose.

I would find her. I was sure of it.

Chapter Seven

The heating had kicked in and the flat was warm when I got up and made some tea and toast Angel sent a text to say she would open up the café at ten, and that most businesses were planning to trade. The thaw made the work of the road-gritting teams easier, and the town would be getting back to normal. Trains and buses were expected back on soon.

I decided to clear my head and walk through town to take out some cash. I showered and dressed quickly in my freshly laundered clothes. I left the flat and took care on the stone steps as they were more slippy than before with their covering of melting ice.

The streets were deep with snow and slush. It was cold, not in the throat numbing way of the last week or so, but moisture hung in the air, and it was misty with dampness. From the top of the steep main street, the view of the far hills was obscured in a mist. I wandered down towards my bank at the bottom of the road, relieved to see most shops opening, and some traffic making it up the now gritted street. It was quieter than normal, the usual sounds of the busy town muffled by snow. The elder townspeople too worried to try to walk, and the younger taking advantage of this unexpected holiday, probably already out with their sledges as the schools hadn't reopened.

I loved the town at this time of year, it looked like a Christmas card scene usually with snow topped hills, church steeples and stone bridges in the distance. Its multi coloured cobbled streets, glinted and glistened in the low winter sun. The town was beautiful, and most businesses had already decorated their shop fronts for the festive season. Leaded glass windows reflected the twinkle of fairy lights against snow and frost. Holly and ivy hung above doorways. At the bottom of the main street I saw council workmen struggle to erect the 10 metre tall tree, and arrange Christmas lights and decorations to drape high across the road and from the lamp posts. The prolonged snow meant they were later than normal though the annual lighting of the tree would go ahead as usual on Saturday afternoon after the traditional Christmas street market which closed off the road for the day and night. As a child I'd loved the feeling of wandering across the road not having to worry about traffic. A feeling came to me that I wouldn't see it this time. I didn't know why.

As I neared the bank, stepping carefully to avoid slippy ice and snow patches, I noticed six or seven women in brightly coloured sports outfits wrapped in scarves, hats and heavy jackets waiting in line on the other side of the road. They were outside a shop I hadn't noticed before. They stamped their feet against the cold, giggling away, their breath hanging around them, with yoga mats under their arms. It was the place where Angel had met Malcolm again. As I watched, an old multi coloured camper van squealed to a stop outside, splashing slush high all around, and a woman jumped out of the cab. I heard her apologising and there were lots of hugs and kisses as the women all embraced and she quickly unlocked the shop and they all pushed in a wild riot of colour against the greying misty day.

Above the shop hung a wooden sign, proclaiming in a Celtic style lettering, the *Body and Spirit Centre*. I blinked in astonishment as I realised that each word was separated by a spiral shape, the same shape I'd seen on the old stones that surrounded the town. Thirteen in total were left, and we'd had one in our garden at the cottage. Tradition said that they had been in place for as long as people had lived in the area. If true it meant thousands of years old. I wanted to know more and as I looked over, the woman popped her head back out of the door, and waved at me. She called over to me and waved again. For a minute I thcught she had to be addressing someone behind me, and I turned to check. There was no one there. She shouted my name

"Kirsty? Kirsty? Do you want to come in? I've got a message for you!"

The shop was a riot of colour, wall hangings, pictures, statues and crystals. I could hear music in a door to one side, and the rest of the room had shelves of books, bowls, statues, and ornaments. It smelled amazing from some smoking incense on the wooden desk which sat in the corner. The woman who had waved to me came back into the room from behind a screen. She was beautiful like a mystical Cleopatra with her black lined green eyes, dressed in a long purple velvet robe, with her red henna coloured hair tied up in a matching band. She looked like she was about to start a ceremony of some kind. Her smile was welcoming and she pulled me into a hug.

"I've heard so much about you Kirsty. Your gran was a real support to me, and taught me so much about local herbs to use in my spells. I am so glad you found me here. Your gran visited me in my meditation this morning. She said you'd come."

What could I say? The whole town seemed to have been taken over by women with spiritual connections. I smiled and tried not to look too shocked.

"I'm JJ." She introduced herself more formally, shaking my gloved hand with hers, bangles and bracelets jingling in welcome

"So delighted to meet you. So delighted. It's an honour Kirsty, I know what you did."

She swung me round to face the closed inner door, missing the shocked expression that flashed across my face.

"Do you want to come in and meet everyone? We've got a class about to start. You'd be very welcome."

"Sorry I don't have any yoga clothes with me." I apologised. "I haven't really experienced yoga. Sorry." I muttered again, shrugging and trying to look more remorseful than I felt.

She laughed, and I had a feeling that she wasn't taken in by my sad face.

"Not a problem Kirsty. We're not doing yoga today", and she threw her head back and laughed loudly as she gently pushed against the door and led me into the room.

"We have a sound therapy session to heal the heart. I think it's perfect for you, and you were delivered by the universe, right on time."

The people I'd noticed outside, all women, were now sitting on the floor in what was a very bright room even though the main window was covered with an orange translucent film. Little electric heaters were plugged in around the white walls, pushing heat towards where everyone reclined on cushions and blankets. A couple of the women chatted, most were quiet, already lying down, relaxing. The room must have been the main shop area at one time, before a partition had gone up to create the entrance space. All around the walls hung multi coloured flags and banners, and pictures of angels and buddhas. I had to admit it wasn't what I expected, though immediately I felt peaceful and a calm settled on me. Like I couldn't help breathe a little deeper and longer.

J.J introduced me as Kirsten's granddaughter and all the women smiled in greeting. It was a warm welcome and some faces I recognised from the shops and the town. As she pushed me towards the back of the room I noticed that they were facing a large copper coloured gong, strung from a wooden frame. It had to be at least about twenty centimetre deep and two metres in circumference and there was a huge wooden stick beside it. J.J changed the music playing through the speakers to a low eastern style chant, with a soft, deep beat. Like a heartbeat. Everyone settled back against their cushions, and the young dark haired woman beside me whispered that I should take off my boots and coat, and make myself comfortable. I pulled a face at that, and she giggled.

"First time?" I nodded and whispered "probably last as well."

"It might seem mad, but it really works. I promise, go with it, and you'll see how good you feel afterwards."

On my other side sat a slightly older woman, she ignored me and seemed to be in a world of her own. She had pulled her greying unwashed hair into a ponytail of sorts, and wore a shabby checked shirt. It looked like a man's shirt and was far too big for her, as were the grey jogging bottoms she wore, sagging around the knees. As I turned towards her I smelt cheap stale cigarette smoke, so strong I pulled back and looked in the other direction. She smelled like she got through a hundred old fags a day. I couldn't help think that she looked really out of place in this white clean space.

"Carol, so good to see you" shouted J.J, and the woman jumped up, and covered her face with her hands, and then with a little gasp, she ran from the room. J.J followed her. I turned to the younger woman beside me, eyebrow raised.

"What's all that about?"

"Carol's mum died last week, so she's still raw. Coming today was really brave of her. She's sole carer for her dad, he has dementia now, and one of her children has autism, another is physically disabled. Her husband died last year, so she's completely on her own now. Her dad smokes like a chimney, and she hates that. She used to be the local head teacher and really into her health and fitness, but she's given up everything to care for family. We all think she's amazing. So these wee workshops really help her, when she can get away. "

I felt ashamed. I had wrinkled up my nose in judgement and she was balancing so many awful situations. No wonder she looked uncared for. When would she get time, and I realised *did it really matter how she looked?*

J.J. re-entered the room, ushering Carol back in, her eyes' wet and red rimmed. A wave of empathy and love so profound I could feel it greeted her from the group, and I could see from her gulp that she was moved. J.J announced that Carol had agreed to treat us all to *toning our chakras,* and the ladies oohed and aahed and settled back down. Carol and J.J sat at the top of the room beside the gong.

I lay back like the others, and cuddled into the blankets and cushions. Not really sure what to expect. I didn't know what toning meant so I followed the others and closed my eyes. The beat from the music reached me, it sounded like a heart beating and I remembered Grizelle's words from last night. Perhaps this was a sign of sorts. J.J instructed us all to take three deep breaths, and to focus on the music. I was already there.

She must have hit the gong because a sound wave so deep and rhythmic hit me slowly. I could only describe it as a tremor moving up my body from my feet to my head. The aftershock remained with me, and then she hit it again, and then again. I had never experienced anything like it, and then Carol started to sing. One note after another, and with the deep boom of the gong the sound was all around me, in me, over me. The physical vibration was such that I couldn't move. I lay there suspended in a space and was only aware that Carol's voice was rising higher and higher, still one note only. As she did so, my mind was full of memories, family, Mum and Dad, Gran and Grandad, Christmas trees, open fires, snow and ice, lots of people around me laughing and joking. I felt part of a bigger group, they moved closer to me, holding me in their arms, whispering in my ear. Happy times, sad times. Tears sprung to my eyes, and above the sound of the singing and the boom of the gong, I could hear women sobbing all around me. With each boom of the gong some of our sadness was released.

I had no idea how long we lay there, it felt eternal. I could hear everything although I was so relaxed I could not move a muscle. I didn't want to. There was something so comforting and accepting about the experience that I wanted it to go on and on. As the last tremor of the gong vibrated around the room, it quietened until there was silence. J.J's voice soft and safe reached me

"Relax and breathe, that's all you have to do, relax and breathe. Take your time, release what needs to be released." She reached over and turned on some music. I could hear an Indian sitar and a female voice chanting "Om shanti Om" over and over again. The sound of the universe Angel had said in the shop. I wandered what that meant. There seemed to be a world going on that I knew nothing about.

I sat up slowly and wiped my eyes, hoping that I hadn't cried out. J.J caught my eye and gestured for me to lie back down, I didn't want to. Instead I sat back on the cushions and dabbed my eyes with my sleeve. I didn't want these strangers to know that I had lost control of my emotions. After a few minutes, the volume of the music turned down, and J.J invited people to share their experiences. A few women talked of visions of their loved ones, and releasing sadness, and how much better they felt as the beamed saintly smiles around the room. I was too embarrassed to say anything yet had to admit to myself that I felt better. Like a weight had lifted.

J.J explained that we can store sadness, grief, shame and other negative emotions in our bodies, in our energy centres, our chakras, and that the toning exercise targets each of those places to release them. The use of the gong was an ancient practice to ease emotions and when that happened we were better able to access our own intuition. It sounded like she was suggesting it was like pressing a reset button, and I liked the sound of that. That when we got past the negative stuff we held on to, we could get back to the essence of who we are. She was watching me intently and I smiled at her so she'd know I was ok. She then offered a comfort break before the workshop resumed and I knew she wanted to talk to me.

"Kirsty can I have a word with you please?" I felt like a guilty schoolgirl caught out breaking the rules. I wondered if she would be angry about me sitting up at the end of the session.

"How was that for you Kirsty?" she asked good naturedly. "Did you enjoy that? The toning and gong can be a bit overwhelming the first time you hear them."

"It was a bit strange, I can't lie" I said, "but I really enjoyed it. For me though, I feel like all I've done is cry for the last few weeks, and if I'd known that would happen I wouldn't have done it. … and now I have done, I feel better, I really do."

J.J beamed at me, and asked me to sit down for a few minutes. She said that she wanted to give me an angel card reading whilst the others relaxed and meditated. There was something in her manner that I knew I couldn't say no, and I could feel her sincerity. Something told me to trust her and I nodded my agreement. She pulled out a heavily embroidered purple pouch from the desk drawer where we sat and took out a set of cards, much larger than playing cards. She blew on them and ran a piece of crystal across the top, before handing them to me and telling me to shuffle.

"It's so your energies go into the cards Kirsty, then we can see what you need to know. Your gran wanted you to feel better about all the stuff you've been carrying. I think that's why you came here today in time for that energy clearing. I need to tell you that you are equipped to do what you are being asked to do. You have to start to believe in yourself more. Trust your intuition, especially now that you've cleared that blocked energy in your heart."

"I don't know how to do that." I said "How do I do it?"

"Let's see what the cards tell us," said J.J "I've got some advice for you, first let's see what the angels want you to know."

She asked me to choose five cards from the pack that she had taken from me and had now spread across the desk top. The gold background on them caught the light, dazzling and dancing. In the background we could hear the rhythmic tone from the music in the other room, and occasional loud girlish laughter. Like they were all young again, or didn't care that their bodies had aged. As we sat she reached behind her and then handed me a piece of a blue-purple amethyst as large as a tennis ball. It matched her dress. "I need to find you a smaller piece as well, to take on your journey." She said. "Amethyst is for protection."

"A journey? And why do I need protection?"

J.J stared off into the distance for a moment, her heavily jewelled right hand hovering over the cards, the many bangles at her wrists rattled together and I was reminded of church bells from what seemed a life time ago. Her hand centred at the large crystal pendant hanging from her neck.

"You know sometimes I say to people who have experienced hardships that it's as if they'd been to hell and back…" She stopped for a moment, and leaned closer to me, her voice a croaky whisper

"This is the first time in twenty years that I mean that. You actually have been to hell and back!" She shivered then, closed her eyes for a moment, and blew out slowly. She looked at me then with admiration in her eyes.

"You really have."

I met her eyes, a silent acknowledgement without the need to say anything else. I felt that if she was genuine then she could see everything she needed to see.

"Kirsty I have to tell you that you will be tested again soon. That it's connected with this journey you are about to take. I've got a message for you, from your grandmother."

I leaned forward. Attentive. Alert.

"The books have gone to where they need to go. Release them. Now always use your intuition, and remember the most important thing. You are loved."

What else would my grandmother say to me? She was an amazing woman, and so wise. That J.J knew about the books was not really a surprise, that Gran wanted me to let them go was.

"You mentioned a journey J.J? Any idea where?" I wondered what she'd say.

"You are crossing water. Ireland. Home. A place you used to know well. Family. Love. It's all there for you."

And then she shivered slightly, and the plume of smoke from burning incense shuddered and changed direction to dance towards a statue of a unicorn which sat on the shelf behind J.J.

"You will be tested though, and when that happens, focus on love. Love from your ancestors, from all who have come before you, to all who will come after."

"I don't like the sound of being tested," I whispered. J.J gestured towards the cards she had turned over.

"It's all there," she said. "Trust in love and follow the signs."

I shook my head and laughed

"I thought fortune tellers were supposed to tell you about love and romance and meeting a tall dark stranger." I said in an attempt to lighten the mood.

"That's all there for you. I told you. There's love for you."

"I thought you meant from family, not romance." I gulped in embarrassment. What if J.J could see everything and knew about my break up and my wish for a love like Angel had? I felt a little shame from that for some reason.

"You've been hurt in the past, now trust me when I say that he was not your soul mate. He is yet to come."

"Can you tell me anything about him?" I whispered, scared in case someone came out of the other room and heard me.

"What can I tell you?" asked J.J as she looked off into the distance again, way beyond the walls of her strange little shop. I knew she wasn't asking me, she posed her question to someone or somewhere else. She looked back at me, seeming to make up her mind, as if agreeing with her source what she could say.

"It's a guy from Glasgow" she said.

I was gutted. Ridiculous as it was it felt like someone had punched me in the guts. A hard jab into my solar plexus. I wasn't winded, I was mad. Mad at myself for listening to it.

All that big build up for a guy from Glasgow? I couldn't help it, my face dropped, and I felt my jaw tighten.

"Don't Kirsty. I promise you. He is your soul mate. You won't be disappointed" I think she could tell from my expression that I wasn't impressed. I was also really annoyed with myself, irritated that I'd cared. This was threatening to overshadow everything else she had told me.

"Have you heard of luminosity?" she asked cutting across my thoughts "To improve your intuition, take heed that if something catches your attention, there's a reason for it. In our fast moving world we tend to ignore things that catch our attention. From now on, what I'd like you to do is that when objects, people, words anything catches your attention take a breath. Take a moment and ask yourself why has this caught your attention. And then wait. It will only take a micro second, a breath, a beat of your heart. It is important to wait. You are waiting for the answer. Do you understand?"

"If something catches my attention I have to ask why? And then wait for an answer?"

"Exactly. It's a guide to follow your intuition. The first thing you have to do is slow down and watch the signs. They always come. We often see or feel the signs and yet we don't take the next step to ask why and then wait for the answer."

I knew what she meant. The previous morning I'd had a feeling about Jane, and I ignored it, and I'd had a thought that Gran's books might get stolen, except I didn't ask who would do it.

"Is it really that simple?" I asked.

"Try it, you'll be amazed with the power we have inside. Release guilt, shame, anger and all the low negative energies, and as you do this you get back to your core. And when things take your attention, people, words, objects, situations, ask the question why have you taken my attention? And then pause for an answer. Life is simple, love is all that matters. Release anything that is not love."

"May I?" she reached for my hands and turned them palms upwards so she could see them, she moved them gently towards the dim light coming in from the street.

"How interesting" she said "you have a simian palm. That's really unusual and your gran had it too!" She looked at me in wonder, pulling my hands closer to the light to improve her view.

"Do you know what that means?" I shrugged I'd never had my palm read before and it seemed a bit ridiculous. I could tell that she was really excited.

"You have it on both hands… and so did your grandmother!!"

"It means that your heart and head lines are merged together so you will find it hard to separate your thoughts and your feelings. It also means that you are a visionary of some kind, and that you have a strong purpose in this world."

Her eyes narrowed again as she looked off into the distance.

"Believe in yourself Kirsty, believe you have a purpose."

Before I could ask anything else, the inner door opened abruptly and the women flooded out in a multi coloured riot of noise and positivity. I felt I had taken up enough of J.J's time and tried to pay her for all her wise counsel. She would not hear of it and instead popped a small piece of deep blue crystal in my pocket.

"For the journey" she whispered in my ear as she hugged and then released me. I left the shop in a bit of a daze. So much to take in and not really knowing where it would all take me. With a deep breath I stopped on the snow edged kerb, water dripping all around me as the day warmed up. A tiny pure white feather floated down past my face. I immediately thought of Angel and Grizelle, and I couldn't help a slight smile. *What had they said?* Angels all around me. That was a nice feeling. I had a sense I would need them.

I forced myself across the road to the bank. One step at a time I thought, cash and euro for my journey. I was going to Ireland, but first, Glasgow and the Druids Temple.

Chapter Eight

I waited a long queue in the bank to change some pounds into euro, my mind racing with all that J.J had said. Around me the talk was of the weather, and all the times before the town had been cut off with snow drifts and ice. It was very hot. The ancient radiators must have been turned up to full capacity so I was relieved to get back outside into the fresher air of the drizzle and misty day. At that moment a bus heading for Glasgow screeched to a halt outside the bank, diesel fumes filling the air. It took only a second to think how convenient that was, before I found myself climbing aboard, paying my fare and taking a seat at the front behind the driver.

The bus was empty of other passengers and we sped along the country roads. Deep snow sitting at the roadside rapidly turned to slush by the newly spread grit. I must have dozed off with the heat of the bus, and within an hour I was at the bus station in Glasgow. As we pulled in I wondered where I could get a bus west towards Clydebank or Helensburgh, a little seaside town on the west coast of Scotland I'd loved as a child, and where Faslane naval base sat. I noticed at the next stance a bus that was heading for Clydebank, the direction I wanted to travel in. *Another sign? This was too easy!*

I asked the driver if he knew the petrol station on Great Western Road, and he nodded and quickly issued me with a ticket, telling me it would take about thirty minutes. He said he would let me know when we reached it. I managed to find a seat close to the front. We were away within a few minutes making our way west through the city streets full of Christmas shoppers. I closed my eyes again and sensed an excitement in my stomach. I was moving closer to something, although I didn't know what.

Progress was slow and it took nearly an hour to reach the suburbs. The driver called out to me and as I got off the bus he pointed to a petrol station on the other side of the road. It was painted blue and yellow, an independent business on a very busy road. Christmas lights and decorations filled the large glass windows facing onto the forecourt. There was also a display of real Christmas trees and ivy wreaths at one side for people to buy. There seemed to be no one around as I walked through and stepped over the low wall at the back. The ground was hard with frost and snow sat at various places all over the land. I hadn't appreciated how high up we were, the view west to the hills was amazing. I could see for miles with no buildings in sight. The sharp wind brought tears to my eyes and I struggled to hold onto my woollen hat. Tightening my scarf around my neck I walked away from the shelter of the building onto the frozen earth and as I did so, the sounds of traffic faded away. All I could hear was the wind singing all around as it lifted the bottom of my coat and tugged at my scarf.

Away in the distance I could see some stones and as I got closer I realised that there were a number of them lying around on the ground in a loose circular shape. The closer I got, the softer the land under my feet became. Although I could see my breath steaming all around me I felt warmer and warmer and within a few minutes of walking I had to loosen my scarf and coat to cool down a bit. Around me I saw little snowdrops on the ground, and tufts of grass coming through, like spring had come early. It was strange because the closer I got to the stones the more signs of plant life I saw.

How amazing I thought, *and so close to Christmas. There must be some kind of underground heat source here.*

After all the temperature had been below zero for days, and I was only about forty miles north of Lanark.

It took me ten minutes or so to finally reach the stones. They were much further than I'd realised. They ranged in size from less than a metre to 3 or 4 metres high, some had fallen over and were lying at angles, half buried in the ground. All were rough and worn, and if they'd ever had any carvings like those close to my home in Lanark, the weather had erased it all away. As much as it had been a pleasant walk, by the time I reached the outlying stones it was as if all my energy had gone and I was drained. I couldn't move another inch. I gratefully slumped down and unbuttoned my coat further, pulling it back and undoing my scarf completely. This unexpected warmth meant I could hardly keep my eyes open. I could have peacefully slept so overcome was I with fatigue.

The petrol station and the wide road were behind me as I sat facing west towards the hills and the setting sun. I noticed a fog move in. Low and slow it curled across the ground, hiding the land bit by bit like someone was rubbing out the landscape, inch by inch. Rock, grass, grit and ground disappeared as it sneaked towards me. So tired I could not move a finger or toe, I could not even blink, and yet I was warm and comfortable to wait. The fog moved closer and I was in such a stupor I imagined that it would be like a warm blanket, comforting and soft and with a feeling of home.

Within minutes I was encased in it and I couldn't see the way back to the roadway. I'd completely lost my bearing so intently had I watched the fog. The strange warmth surrounded me, nurtured me, and my eye lids were heavy in my head. I had no fear, and yet part of me was aware of my situation. My rational mind told me that I'd get lost if I moved. And although it made perfect sense to wait, to stay in the same spot and not wander off, another part of me knew it was an excuse. I could not have moved if I'd wanted to. If even my life depended on it. How close to the truth was that. Realistically I knew I'd have to wait for the mist to lift. A moment of clarity hit me. *What on earth had I done in this mad weather, and so close to darkness as well. Who could help me here?*

I had no sooner thought that when I heard a voice calling out

"Hello. Hello. Are you there?"

It sounded like an old voice, croaked yet deep and strong, and within a few seconds he appeared out of the fog. A very old man walked towards me, dressed in a tweed suit, wearing a cloth flat cap, and using a walking stick to ease his passage across the awkward ground. His white hair had grown long past his collar and he had long side whiskers, and bushy eyebrows. Close up I saw he had the chain of a pocket watch tucked into his waistcoat pocket. He wore no scarf nor gloves, as if he too was feeling the heat from this place.

He saw me and his face broke into a beaming smile.

"You are well my child? I hope I did not startle you?"

He settled down on a stone, which looked like it had been carved into a throne by ancient hands. Like an old monarch from a bye gone age he gestured with his cane for me to take a place on a smaller stone beside him. It hugged me as if it had been cut to fit against my body, holding me upright as by that time I would have gratefully lay down and slept.

"Wrap yourself up. Its cold outside you know. Don't want you catching a chill."

I wasn't sure if he was confused or not, and for a moment I wondered if he had wandered out from a nursing home. Unless he was wearing thermal underwear he didn't appear to be dressed for the weather. He turned to me with bright alert eyes and said "Did you know there's a Druid's Temple here?"

"That's why I came." I told him. "I wanted to find it, but I was told they'd built the petrol station on it."

"On some of it." He said ".....the energy of it remains. May I show you it my child?"

I felt I could trust him, and I nodded my head.

"Yes please, if you can. Before you do, can I ask you something?" He nodded his head "Do you know a woman called Jane? She said she's from here and I think she has some books of mine. I'd like to get them back."

"I do know her" he said. 'She's not far from here, let me ask you something first? Why do you want to have them back? Are you planning to use them? Or to hold on to them for evermore? Do you need them or do you want them? Would you feel differently if you knew they've gone to where they need to be?" His eyes twinkled at me, and I heard my gran's voice in my head.

"Release what you don't need." She had said. The warmth, the reassurance and the need to keep this old man happy had me agreeing.

"Release what you don't need." He whispered as she had done in my mind. "Now let me tell you about the Temple." He pointed with his stick, back towards the direction he'd come from. As he did so I noticed that the fog moved back quickly as if his cane had directed it and it had to do his bidding.

"Can you imagine" he said "five thousand years ago, how special this place was. People worked together side by side with a common purpose. To build a temple here on this land, where the sky reaches the earth and the waters of the Clyde estuary kept the area fertile and abundant. We now call them Druids. They were special people and others called them that in the language of their times 'doine sidh' people of the mounds. Some believe they came from within the earth to live here amongst men. All we know is that they understood the land and all that lived on her. They had special gifts of healing, of working with nature and animals, and used their powers wisely. For them their purpose in life was to serve the land, and in doing so, they served their fellowship. They travelled for many miles guided by their connection with the stars and their own inner knowing to find this special place. They used only the local materials, timber, mud, and willow canes to build a temple which is why nothing physical remains except its imprint upon this land."

As he spoke something strange happened to me. It was as if I could see shadows in the mist, men, women and children dressed in long robes, moving around in the distance. Ghosts from the past and for a moment I wondered if I'd happened upon a film set or historical re-enactment. It felt that real.

" ...the temple was very large" he continued using his stick to draw patterns in the frosted earth, exposing a deep red sand beneath, like he was cutting across flesh. I shivered again.

"Can you imagine it? The temple would have been as big as three football pitches, with many inner temples within. All with their own designs from the landscape. At its heart was the labyrinth. The place of power and one that transcended this third dimensional place called earth. To walk the labyrinth was a great honour, entrusted to only a few. Those men and women who had left ego behind and who could be best trusted with power."

He leaned closer to me and whispered "Have you heard of this before?" I shook my head. "No, it sounds magical." I whispered back to him.

I leaned closer, to better hear his whispers and watch as his cane continued to cut across the ground. He drew snakes and dragons and unicorns and the sun, moon and stars. With his words I glanced upwards and saw each star burning bright against the coal black night sky. I imagined if I were to draw a line from star to star what the shape would be. I knew it would be a familiar symbol.

He talked about an underground kingdom, a place holding what he called the Giants of Old, and the work done by the elementals, beings of the earth. All the while whispering in my ear of its magic and power. I was mesmerised, and the feeling was strange. In an odd type of hypnosis and yet oblivious to the passage of time and the sleet shower which settled all around us.

My idyll was ruined by an angry loud blast of a horn from the traffic behind me. And with that intrusion I sat up fast, frozen and feeling disorientated like I'd woken from one of my nightmares. I was extremely cold and quickly tightened my scarf, pulling my coat tight around me. I only turned to glimpse the road for a breath, and yet in that time the old man had gone. I heard the clicking of his cane as he slipped away in the darkness. I couldn't see him. I called out. Hoping that he'd appear again. He didn't come back. The dark had swallowed him leaving nothing behind, not even a shadow. I shook my head as it was like waking from a dream so entranced had I been with the stories of the temple and the Druids.

It was then I felt the numbness in my body, each nerve ending stabbed with burning hot pokers as I started to move. Despite tightening my scarf and coat as bidden by the old man, I was frozen. Colder than I'd ever felt in my life. I could see icicles hanging from my exposed hair. Frost had settled on my coat and lap as I'd sat on the stones. My head throbbed. My throat was dry and my lips chapped and raw from the blast of the icy winds. Yet again I felt foolish, to succumb to the Scottish winter elements so close to a main road was laughable. It seemed stupid, and I told myself that many times as I walked very slowly and stiffly back towards the lights of the road and petrol station.

My fingers were too sore to unzip my pocket to find my phone and use the torch, and I was also worried that I'd drop it and lose it forever or break it. So I took my time carefully picking my way over the frozen, uneven ground, feeling every bump against my sore feet. It took me ages to hobble across to the low wall. Two men in overalls rushed towards me, and offered very welcome helping hands as I climbed over, legs still numb and tight. They smiled and laughed and the oldest one said,

"We were going to send out a search party for you young lady! We were getting worried there."

The younger man, darker than the other, addressed me, nodding over to the shop doorway,

"Pop into the shop and get warmed up, Audrey has some coffee ready for you."

I squinted against the harshness of the bright overhead lights, they looked similar, probably father and son. From their manner I guessed they owned or managed the site.

"Go on my dear" said the older man. "My daughter has a drink ready for you. She's been worried about you, sitting over at those stones on your own all this time. She said she was giving you another five minutes then she was coming to get you."

They both laughed again, and turned and pointed towards the shop.

"Thanks...." I realised I was struggling to speak, my throat was dry and raw. "That's really kind of you..... But I wasn't on my own. I was talking to an old man....'"

The look that passed between the two men stopped me saying more.

"No hen," said the younger man, in the local endearment for a woman, "you've been on your own, and we've been watching you for the last hour. We saw you heading over to the stones, and you've sat on your own there. Look we've got a great view from here. We've been cleaning this pump all day."

"What about the fog? Maybe you didn't see him in the fog?"

Again that look between them, quick, concerned, sad.

"It's been a right miserable day...." said the elder man, "There hasn't been any fog, pet. It's been clear all afternoon. And you've been sitting there for the last hour. On your own."

Chapter Nine

Such a strange feeling I'd had, like in a dream. The whole experience hadn't seemed real. However, my frozen aching body told me that I had spent ages sitting outside, in the midst of the Scottish winter. I must have looked drunk as I staggered forward and pushed open the shop doorway. Christmas music hit me with its loud joyfulness and I halted for a moment, my senses overwhelmed with the noise and the light. This had happened to me a lot recently. Like the noise of life was too much for me at times.

A dark haired woman about my age was behind the counter and she looked at me closely as I came to a sudden stop. She smiled, and nodded towards the back of the shop where I could see a sign for the ladies toilet. The fluorescent tube dazzled my eyes and harshly illuminated the small space. I looked in the mirror and saw what a sight I was. A pale faced ghost, mascara around my eyes and hair like frozen candy floss. I washed my hands and stood for a few minutes with the hot air dryer blowing on my head. In an attempt to warm up.

Had I imagined the whole thing? The old man? The fog? How could I have made up the labyrinth or the Giants of Old? I'd never heard of either. Something strange had happened to me out there. I needed to know more. Whatever had happened I had a strange feeling. Something deep inside me was calling again. Only a little voice, it was strong and it felt right. I needed to find out about the labyrinth and the Druids, and the Giants of Old. I wished my grandmother was still here. She would have known. In her place I knew who I could ask. I hoped Grizelle was still in Lanark as I really wanted to know more, and she knew everything.

Or maybe your dad can help a voice inside my head whispered.

I was still shaking my head as I re-entered the main shop. The girl behind the counter looked relieved when she saw me.

"Here I've poured you a coffee. Hope this warms you up!" She smiled in greeting and looked so kind. Like an angel as she stood amongst the Christmas fairy light, with tinsel glowing all around her.

"Audrey?... eh, thanks. That's really kind of you. I really need this. Your Dad?..." I paused to make sure, she nodded in agreement

"....and my brother Michael." She added.

"Like the Arch-angel? "She grinned and pulled a face "...both were really helpful there. I thought I'd been outside for ages. It seemed like that...."

"Perhaps because it's already so dark?" She suggested "In this weather you don't want to be out too long. Especially sitting on the stones. I tend to sit there in the summer for my lunch break. It's got an amazing feeling over there. Hasn't it? Almost like you're in a different world."

"Yes, yes. That's what it was like.... like I was in a different world." I took a quick glance at her before I whispered. "Have you ever seen anyone there?"

She laughed "Like the king of the fairies?" Perhaps it was the look on my face, perhaps it was something else, she stared at me, deeply, like she was about to tell me something, before anything more was said, the bell over the door tinkled and a couple of customers came in to pay for their petrol and buy some sweets. Making small talk and pleasantries with Audrey, I withdrew to the side of the coffee counter, and helped myself to a latte from the self-service machine. I picked up some chocolate and took it all to the counter as they left.

"What made you say *the king of the fairies*" I asked as soon as we were alone again.

"Och nothing" she said, nodding her head "just my wee day dreams from when I was younger. It probably sounds mad, only Dad really got it. My mum said it was daft."

I nodded to encourage her, hoping she'd share more.

"I used to dream that the king of the fairies came out to see me and he'd lead me dancing in and out the stones around and around like we were making spiral shapes, and all the little fairies and creatures would be dancing and singing. It was fun and it had me laughing all the time. My mum said it was daft, my dad said to take care that they didn't lead me laughing into their fairy kingdom, because then I'd never come home." She laughed again, shaking her head, her brown eyes bright, glancing at me to see if I thought that too.

The door bell sounded again, and her dad came into the shop. He smiled at us both with such a kind face and nodded towards me

"I've just heard that the buses are finished for the day. There's some really bad weather coming in. Audrey do you want to take our friend here into town?"

She smiled and immediately agreed, pulling on a heavy parka as she strode out of the shop. Before I had time to say anything I was climbing beside her into a big four wheel drive break down truck. Coffee and chocolate still in my hands, she laughed off my attempts to pay.

"You heard the boss." She laughed again, "he wouldn't have left you stranded out there. We need to get you back. Now where's best? Is the city centre ok?"

I told her I'd try and get the train back to Lanark, in case the buses to Lanarkshire were also off, so Glasgow Central Station would be ideal. As we headed towards the city centre we could see the road in front of us like a ribbon of sparkling light with the reflection of the street lights and the frost surrounding us. Snow clouds blotted out the stars above, and despite the heat from the blowers within the van, I shivered.

Audrey glanced sideways at me as she expertly handled the truck. For some reason she started to tell me about her relationship with her dad. Her mum had died ten years before, and her small family were all close, running the business together. Her Dad and brother were mechanics and ran the breakdown service, she managed the shop and petrol station side of the business. She was telling me about the special bond she had with her dad, how he was kind, caring and always compassionate. I felt a tear run down my face, and she spotted it before I could wipe it away.

"Tell me about your dad" she said, and I found myself sharing all I knew and all I could remember with this stranger in the darkened cab. Something I'd never have imagined I would do. I told her of the sadness I felt that I didn't know him, and the shame I had of losing contact with him years and years ago. That I hadn't thought of him for such a long time until Gran's death, and that I used to let people assume he was dead. And that had become the story I told myself. I finished with telling her of the strange dreams I was having, and that I'd had a call from him after the funeral, asking me to help him. It was strange to unburden myself in this way, like the darkened cab was a church confessional box. Tears flowed again, and Audrey passed me a tissue, silently. I felt her sympathy.

"Obviously I don't know your dad" she said, "I don't know what I would have done without mine. We have an incredible bond. I can always rely on him. He has made me. I can't imagine what it would have been like without him. You owe it to yourself to find him, and make amends if you have to. He's your dad. You won't need to do a thing. I promise. Just find him, and don't leave it any longer. You're part of him, he's part of you."

I could feel the truth in her words. It just felt right. The tears stopped, and my voice felt stronger.

"Yes, I'll do it. I'm going to book a flight to Ireland and find him." She glanced at me again, just as we turned into Hope Street, and then took another right hand turn into the eerily quiet drop off point at the station.

"Last time I went to Ireland, it was with my dad" she said, "we got the train and the ferry. I loved the journey, much better than flying. "

As I opened the door, the overhead light flicked on and I saw her eyes looking towards the brightly lit ticket office, even though her vision was full of memories from a long time ago.

"It was a great journey, probably the best holiday we ever had. I'm glad we didn't fly."

There was something in what she said or the way she said it that I felt in my body. I was supposed to take note of it in some way, the moment passed. We said our goodbyes and she refused any money towards petrol or the coffee or chocolate with the usual Scottish *put your purse away* and that made us both laugh. She called "I sound like my granny now!" as she pulled away and headed back across the icy roads, and that made me laugh again. I had a warm sensation in my heart and I felt my gran close to me as I slipped my way into the station.

People were running around in the brightly lit station, panicked and frustrated with the long queues of fellow cold and angry passengers at the ticket machines. No doubt trying to get close to home since their buses had been cancelled. I checked the board and saw that the Lanark train would leave in thirty minutes, time to visit the travel centre, and hope I'd make it back ok. Like so many of the main train stations in Scotland, it was a large Victorian built building. Thick sandstone arches soared high holding up the glass roof above the twenty or so platforms. The damp smell of diesel hit me, against a background of coffee and frying chips, and wet wool coats. Part of the station floor had been resurfaced with a rubber tile effect oddly slippy when wet, which was very strange in a country of rain. People were slipping and sliding both inside and outside the station. The electronic noticeboard sat above the metal ticket barriers to platforms 1 to 8. The London train left from Platform 1, the Lanark train from Platform 4. So close together and yet offering two very different lives for me.

The ticket office was at the front of the station, so I turned back and pushed open its heavy glass door. It was quiet, the floor covered with timetables, receipts and travel magazines, ripped into pieces. Like a paper tsunami had rushed through. Only one of the red window blinds was open, and the large man I could see there was counting cash, uniform jacket thrown untidily on the back of his chair, sleeves rolled up.

"Sorry we're closed." A woman shouted over as she moved behind me to flip the sign on the door. The man looked up and I smiled hoping that he wouldn't throw me out before I had some information.

"Can I help you?" he asked. "It's been crazy here for the last hour. We should have closed thirty minutes ago."

"I was wondering how much it would cost to go to Ireland" I said "and when the next train would be."

His face broke into a smile and he laughed. "You're too late" he said

"For Ireland, I mean."

"Because of the snow?" I asked.

"Eh, naw hen", he addressed me informally. "The ash cloud! Have you no heard?"

He could tell from my expression that I didn't know anything. Two of his colleagues joined him to dramatically explain all they had learned in the last hour or so. They excitedly spoke over each other as they rushed to tell me that an Icelandic volcano had erupted and spat thousands of tons of ash and rock into the atmosphere, grounding all air traffic in most of Western Europe and North America. For the train station it meant in the last hour they had fielded hundreds of enquiries for rail and ferry tickets as people hastily tried to change their travel arrangements.

It seemed unbelievable, and I realised that it put paid to any plans of mine to travel to Ireland in the foreseeable future. Disappointment hit me in the stomach like a clenched fist. How could they miss seeing that reaction as it played across my face. "How long is it likely to last?"

Two of the men folded their arms, leaning back against the glass, like navy blue bookends in their railway uniforms, shaking their heads, the other scratched his. They shared in the drama. "No idea". "Don't know". "Who knows". They all exclaimed at the same time.

The first man I'd spoken to leaned forward.

"Are you on your own?" He asked. My eyes filled with sad tears and I couldn't resist a loud and unladylike sniff as I nodded. Silently pleading with him for help.

"Where was it you wanted to go?" He asked. I told him I was trying to get to Newgrange and thought Drogheda was the nearest town to it. I couldn't help that my voice wobbled a bit. I really felt disappointed, and annoyed at myself. If I hadn't gone or stayed as long at the temple site, I'd have known all about the volcano and would have had my ticket booked. I should have noticed what Grizelle had said yesterday I remembered. She'd said something about flight problems, she must have known somehow. She was so connected and now it was too late and I wouldn't get to Ireland, or have the chance to find my dad. Everything Audrey had said about her relationship with her dad sounded in my head.

His face broke into a big smile.

"That's where my dad is from." He said proudly.

"Mine too." I knew it would be fine at that. I could feel something change.

"Let me check again." He offered kindly, even though his fellow workers were shaking their heads.

"Getting a seat on the ferry is the main thing. It's a busy time anyway and with this it's been crazy. When can you travel?"

I told him anytime. It wasn't like I wanted to be there for Christmas like other people, and there really wasn't any need to either wait or worry about getting back for anything specific. He puffed out his breath, cheeks pink with effort as he started typing into his machine.

"Tomorrow?" He asked as he jabbed at his keyboard with his two thick index fingers, his tongue sticking out, his shirt collar unbuttoned, tie loosened with relief at the end of his shift, or so he had thought.

"I don't believe this look, its offering me the last seat on tomorrow morning's ferry. Someone must be looking after you hen. I'm sure I checked that earlier and it was full. You need to be on the 7.30am train from here though can you make it back into the town for then?"

The other two workers were obviously shocked, and yet delighted for me. Shaking heads they kept saying that it was unbelievable. I bought an open dated return and included the Lanark to Glasgow part as well. It would mean an early start, and with any luck I'd be in Drogheda for dinner time.

Home. A little voice whispered deep inside me. *Dad. I'm coming home.*

<u>Chapter Ten</u>

I made it back to Lanark without any further delays, and luckily for me a taxi was waiting at the rank and didn't mind taking me round to the cottage, where he waited whilst I hastily packed a bag for my trip. The driver proudly told me he had fitted snow tires to his vehicle which meant he could work when his competition was off the road. I didn't have the heart to tell him that if our road hadn't been cleared by the local farmer, snow tires wouldn't have made a difference.

The cottage had been icy even though I'd kept my coat on and ran through it like a maniac. I was so very relieved to get dropped off at Angel's warm house again. I took my time yet I still slipped on the outside stone stairs as I climbed to her flat. She'd left some soup, bread and butter, and my favourite carrot cake out on the counter top, with a wee welcoming note. As I stretched out in front of the stove, she phoned to check I was ok, and I quickly filled her in on my day. The sound healing session, the experience at the stones with the invisible old man, and booking my tickets because of the volcanic ash cloud. She chuckled when I described the man and all he'd told me.

"Sounds like an ancient mystic, a Druid to me. Only you could see him because his message was for you and you were a seeker or *Firrin Sealgair* as your gran would say a *truth hunter.* Have you heard about Merlin?" She asked. "We might laugh now about legends but I've found that the supernatural world has its own laws. I've been reading a lot about Merlin recently why couldn't it be him there to take you on another adventure?"

"Adventure, Angel?" I shrieked "I thought I was going to die the last time! Please don't wish anything like that on me again."

"Kirsty, you are not the woman you were. You can cope with anything. I strongly believe that we only get what we can cope with. You are a truth hunter, a spiritual truth hunter and you can cope with much more than you give yourself credit for."

She took a deep breath before she continued. "Your gran was the same, as was your dad and his line. It will be good for you to connect with them. I hear they were healers."

This was the first I'd heard. "Angel why have you not told me this before?" I asked.

"I wasn't sure when or what to tell you." She eventually whispered. "You'll get the full story soon enough."

"I'm not even sure if he'll be at Newgrange." I confessed. "He hasn't called back and when I try to call it, the number rings out. I'm probably going on a wild goose chase, and now you're talking about Merlin? I don't know what to say. It sounds mad."

"Madder than hell?" she asked.

She was right. What did I know about any of my recent experiences?

"What does your intuition tell you?" she asked.

I let out a long low breath. I had to go. I didn't know why, I had to get to Newgrange. I told her and she agreed, telling me to trust in myself. It was the kind of thing gran would have said.

"Is Grizelle still around?" I asked "I wondered if she would know more about the things the old man said."

"She left late last night with her friend Maggie from the peace camp. Do you remember her? They'll be on their vessel by now. She was so right about the flights wasn't she?"

"I was thinking that earlier. How could she have known that? Actually, stupid question, why wouldn't she have known given she is so connected."

"I meant to say, there was something about the other night when we all left."

"Uh huh."

"Something I feel I missed and I don't know what it was."

"Like what?" She asked, giving nothing away.

"About Grizelle I wondered when she got so friendly with Maggie from the camp?"

There was a pause. "Angel?"

"She would probably have preferred to say herself, but its early days.......... in their *relationship.*"

It took a moment or two to sink in. "So she's a le....... she's in a *relationship* with Maggie?" That I wasn't expecting.

"I don't know why I'm so shocked. What a woman! Nearly eighty and she's in love with a woman. Good for her."

My admiration for Grizelle soared. I could hear Angel laughing.

"I'm delighted for her. As I said it's early days, and after all they are both well over twenty one."

She was still laughing as we said goodnight, and wished me well, telling me to ask the angels for help if I needed it, although as she also said, my loved ones were always with me. *Truth hunter* I liked the sound of that, even if I didn't know why, and descended from Irish healers. I searched for that quickly on my phone and fell asleep reading about healing abilities coming from faeries in a place underground called the Other World, and how truth was a magical force always upheld by the king. The warmth of the flat and the good food meant I slept soundly until my alarm rang at 5am.

I sent Grizelle a short text asking about labyrinths and if she knew of the Giants of Old, and telling her that I thought she and Maggie were perfect for each other. There was something else she'd said that niggled at me, it wouldn't come to the surface. I hadn't received a reply by the time I left to catch the 06.20 train, hoping it wouldn't be delayed. I was relieved when the train pulled into Glasgow Central station, only a few minutes behind schedule. The journey had passed in a blur of snow filled gardens and parkland. I had always loved that train journey. With only a few minutes to change platforms, I hurried along the wet and slippy concourse and found a seat on the packed 7.30 am train to Ayr, an old seaside town on the Ayrshire coast. My ticket included a coach connection from there to Cairnryan where we would catch the ferry to Belfast. Once in Belfast I would have to find the train station to take me south towards Drogheda.

I was excited, sitting there with my bag on my knee, squeezed in with a variety of travellers. Most looked around them in amazement, probably used to flying from Glasgow to Belfast, and not this older means of travel. I wondered about my dad and the journeys he must have made over the years. How he and mum had met, I didn't even know or remember that story. *Surely I should have known that?*

A little red haired Irish girl caught my attention. Clutching a teddy bear, her other hand held tightly to her proud daddy. Dressed in a pink coat with fake pink fur around her wee face, she looked worried even as her adoring daddy tried to coax a smile out of her. It was so cute I looked around the carriage to see if anyone else was as entranced as I was. A young couple held hands and had eyes only for each other, a pregnant lady smiled at the scene, and an older couple also seemed dreamily taking it in, like it reminded them of their young family and happy times. We all smiled that way you do to strangers before turning back to travel companions, books, magazines or mobile phones. That's what I did until we arrived at Ayr. Another once grandly built train station. Very polite commuters stood aside to let us disembark, everyone heading outside into the weak, welcome seaside sunshine. It felt much milder than Glasgow, and I hoped that would mean the road trip to the ferry terminal and the crossing would be easy. A sense of uneasiness settled over me at that point. That annoying little voice whispered *no it won't*.

A queue of about twenty people stood waiting for the doors to open to the white coach which sat belching out diesel fumes on the station forecourt, mixing painfully with the smell of the sea. Huge gulls called loudly overhead. Even at this time in the morning I could smell fish and chips. The driver was very pleasant and professional as he shepherded us on to the bus, saying that as it was so busy we'd have to put luggage in the compartment under the bus. A short argument broke out between a middle aged couple who looked like they were carrying their worldly belongings. The woman was adamant she wasn't letting anything out of her sight. The driver interceded by saying that she would be welcome to travel in the baggage hold if she wanted. This seemed to make up her mind and she trounced away from the husband, leaving him to stow it all away. I was quite glad to drop my bag off, and joined the queue. Within minutes we were all on board, I found myself sitting beside the little girl and her daddy. Both were asleep before the bus set off on what I was relieved to see, were snow free roads and bright blue sky ahead.

The bus journey should have lasted nearly two hours on the winding coastal road through slow vacant villages. The early start caught up with me and I too must have dozed off in the warmth, with the heaters on full, steaming up the windows forcing lethargy in all. I woke with a start to find us at a standstill, chilled air from the open doors forcing its way in, and people talking all around me. The bus had broken down, and we were waiting for a replacement to come up from the ferry terminal. It's funny how people react differently when things like that happen. There were a couple of folk who took the opportunity to stretch their legs outside the bus, some needing to smoke. There were those who moaned and complained that we were bound to miss the ferry, others who sat in tension and said nothing. I sat back, and focused on the view. In the distance I could see the sea loch from where the ferry would leave. The water was the colour of charcoal, and the sky overhead had darkened down, black cloud sat low. A bumpy crossing was in store for us whenever we reached the ferry. There was nothing I could do, so I breathed deep and tried to relax. There was no point in stressing myself out, and we didn't know what was happening or how long we'd be there. I reasoned that the company would want to get us going as fast as they could. The bus was still warm, the seats comfortable enough, so for the moment we weren't in any danger of freezing to death. From the corner of my eye I saw what looked like a white feather fall past the window.

"Look Daddy," called out the little red haired girl, "an angel said we'd be fine and not to worry!"

This had almost everyone laughing out, and the little girl buried her head in her daddy's shoulder, embarrassed at the attention her outburst had attracted. However only a couple of minutes later, the driver called in to us that he could see the other bus coming up the steep hill and we'd be swapped over soon. A half-hearted cheer rang out. We all got our things together, and sure enough were on board the replacement bus and on our way quickly afterwards. Sleet hit off the windows as we rounded the last hill and headed down towards the port. I was now sitting at the front of the new bus and could see a ferry rolling with the waves. I sent up a silent prayer *please don't let it be too bumpy a crossing*. It had been years since I'd been on water and this didn't look good.

We grabbed our bags as quickly as we could, the wind whipped our faces, hard sleet blinding our vision. I looked back towards the hills, a mist had rolled in low and silent. I shivered again, remembering my experience at the stones. I hoped this wasn't another sign.

Chapter Eleven

The ferry was huge, much bigger than I'd imagined, as tall and vast as a building. It towered over the terminal. Lorries and trucks already disappearing into its vast belly. It pushed and pulled against its steel shackles as if desperate to get back to the ocean. We were guided into the building through automatic glass doors, permanently opened with the gasping wind that blew us forward. On the other side of a rope barrier people were disembarking. The stench of vomit hit me, and I had to take a step backwards. So many people helping and being helped off the boat. Looking around them, relieved, exhausted, legs wobbly on dry land. It must have been a terrible crossing.

I gulped back nausea from the fumes of diesel and the rest of the smells trapped in the building, it rose, burning the back of my throat. I wasn't a good traveller, and knew there was no going back. With a deep breath I dropped off my bag on the conveyor belt, showed my ticket and waited in line for the doors to open onto the enclosed bridge to take us to the boat. A small blonde woman in a security uniform apologised for the delay. She said additional cleaning had been required, as the sailing over from Belfast had been "really bad." This was delivered with a wrinkling of her nose and her eyes screwing up. I didn't mind too much, I was happy to prolong departure for as long as possible, unlike others around me. I could feel their anxiety levels rising with each additional minute that passed.

We waited nearly twenty minutes before the doors opened automatically and we were able to walk up the incline to the passenger bridge taking us to the heart of the boat. The stairwell was painted in a light pastel blue, with modern art works arranged tastefully. However, I still found it tight and oppressive. Lighting was low in an attempt to calm passengers down perhaps, and I saw the signs for shops, cafes, cinema, and even a spa, which surprised me greatly. I had no idea it was going to be so big.

Without my bag I was free to wander the ship. Fellow passengers seemed to know where they were going and followed the smell of food to the restaurants and coffee shops. My stomach hadn't quite recovered though, and I was worried about being sick on the crossing, so I headed further upstairs and followed the signs out on to the deck.

Pushing the heavy door open took a lot of effort, as if an unseen force of nature battled against me to hold it close. It took a supreme effort to push it open and I staggered out onto the deck area. Luckily for me one of the crew was on the other side, and managed to grab my arm as I slipped and almost fell. The boat unstable as it reared back and forward anxious to get away, banging against the sides of the quay. He was a much older man, with a thatch of white hair and a huge handlebar moustache to match. I mouthed my thanks as the wind whipped away any sound apart from the roar of the engines, and his eyes twinkled as he wandered off to the other side of the structure, his yellow waterproof jacket parachuting around him. He paused for a moment and then battled his way back towards me, and with a wink he said.

"I forgot to say don't forget to give a homage to Neptune now! The God of the Seas. That'll help us all!"

He shouted into my ear, and then with a laugh and another wink he was away again. Leaving me standing all alone, swaying back and forward with the wind. There was no one else mad enough to be out there and I worked my way up the boat, struggling at times to hold on to the wet hand rails and stay upright on the slippy steel underfoot. From deck to deck I wandered finding it was easier to stand on the shore side in the shelter from the voracious wind, continually having to hold onto my woollen hat to stop it being ripped from my head. Behind us a black cloud had settled over the hills that disappeared into a mist that had fallen from the sky. I heard a horn blow so loud I jumped. The hydraulics tethering the steel cables to shore roared, and the huge boat rocked from side to side as it left its moorings behind. Heading up the hillside road away from the port glowed the red tail lights of hundreds of cars and lorries, on their way to Scotland after their traumatic journey. I hoped the weather on dry land was an improvement on their journey over.

The ferry rocked again, and I had to hold on tight to the rails to keep my balance as it was very slippy underfoot from the sleet which settled around us. Grasping the rail, despite my thick gloves I felt the chill and damp. As we headed north out of the deep water haven of Loch Ryan, the ship's horn blew again and a screeching voice gave instructions on safety on board. Outside in the frigid air I only grasped a few words before they were carried off by the wind. The acrid smell of diesel mixed with the fishy smell of the sea and the roll of the ground beneath my feet meant I vomited violently over the side. Thankful that the wind whipped it away from me. My stomach spasmed painfully again and again. Until there was nothing left, my throat was raw, my guts ached, my breath was rank and I felt like my teeth would dissolve. In my pocket I found a tissue to wipe my mouth and some chewing gum and sat down on one of the benches, still in the lea of the boat as it shuddered and turned to brace against nature's onslaught. The wet seat chilled my legs, yet there was no way I was leaving the fresh biting air, at least until I could trust my tummy not to empty unexpectedly. I wondered how Grizelle was dealing with the North Sea, surely that had to be worse than this. As I thought of her I couldn't help smile, she was probably commanding the seas to quieten. A vision of her standing at the front of an old smelly fishing boat came to my mind. Like Neptune, holding aloft a trident, tweed cape flowing behind her in the wind.

I sent up a prayer to the Angels, like I'd done before.

Please, please, please make this boat stop rocking.

A little white feather sat beside me on the steel seat and I felt a slow warmth spread across my body. After a few long deep breaths my panic subsided. I remembered what the man had said about Neptune and felt round in my pocket. They were empty apart from the purple blue amethyst stone J.J. had given me "for the journey" she had said and I most definitely needed some help for this part of the journey. I tentatively took the stone from my pocket, holding it up to the light. It sparkled and in it I could see a million shades of blue. A reflection of the darkest sea to the lightest sky. I took a moment and steadied myself with another deep breath. I wasn't sure if there was anything I needed to say, as looking around me I would have felt self-conscious as some people had joined me up on the deck. All looked queasy though, and well wrapped up against the weather. Despite my hat, coat, scarf and gloves, the bitter sleet that landed on my bare face burned like ice against my skin. My nose had lost all feeling, and my cheeks ached against the damp chilled air of the December day. I still didn't want to take the chance of returning inside. I didn't want the humiliation of vomiting amongst the seats of the lounge, or dining room. That would have been awful so I remained outside leaning miserably against the metal rails trying to see through the drizzle towards the open sea and Ireland. I popped the crystal over the side and thanked Neptune for the fabulous voyage I was about to have. Almost immediately I had a feeling of excitement about Ireland with still so many questions to be answered. The engines roared even louder as if they were fighting to find more power, the boat moved direction and all around me people slipped and slid along the deck, rushing to hold on. I glanced quickly towards the noise, and with that the stench of marine diesel hit me and my whole stomach bounced again. Acrid bile bit the back of my throat and I dreaded vomiting again. Holding tight to the railings I breathed deeply through my mouth, willing the ship to straighten out. I sent up a little prayer for help and closed my eyes, trying not to cry. This was hopeless I felt wretched and we hadn't even cleared Loch Ryan yet.

What would I be like at the end of this four hour journey?

As I opened my eyes again, the boat lilted as it left the sea loch behind with promises of a safe return as it blasted three times with its horn, and headed into the Irish Sea. Waves and spray covered the deck and a few of us had to move back quickly into the shelter of the structure to avoid the water. As I did so a most delicious fragrance reached my nostrils, and like a thirst in a desert, I latched on to it. I didn't recognise it but needed to focus as it took my awareness away from diesel. It smelled musky and masculine, a male eau de toilette or after shave, and I instinctively turned towards its source.

To my right I was aware of the appearance of a tall broad figure. He was looking out to sea, and leaned against the steel railing, close to me. Slipping and sliding on the deck it was hard not to bump into each other. He apologised, and as I looked up in acknowledgement I was struck by the dazzle from bright blue eyes under dark brows. His face tanned, straight nose, white teeth. A really handsome man who smelled beautifully. I laughed self-consciously instantly aware of my sickly demeanour and hoping he hadn't witnessed my vomiting earlier. I could hear my friend Jen's voice in my head. "Seize the Day" she used to say, and that made me smile more widely at him. I hoped my teeth were clean.

He apologised again for bumping into me, and explained that it was bound to get bumpier now that we were in open water. One look at my face and he must have realised that I wasn't a good traveller, and he sort of guided me towards the stairs and up another flight, telling me that he'd find me somewhere more sheltered to stand and that we should get away from the diesel. I was so grateful for his company, and his gorgeous face that if he'd suggested I jump into the sea I might have nodded eagerly and done so. It was with relief that I realised that he was right. At the top of the boat, protected from the sleet and wind there was a calmness. Looking around I saw some people I recognised from the train and bus, including the little girl and her daddy. He had dressed both of them in clear waterproof jackets, the kind that pack into a pocket, and he was holding her tight to him. I was distracted for a moment. A little memory bounced about in my head of an earlier journey I must have done with my daddy. Looking down I saw little red wellingtons, I was wearing a red coat, with a hood. He had me up on his shoulders, my fingers in his thick dark curly hair. A tear came into my eye, of sadness, recognition, loss, loneliness and I turned away from my new companion.

He had noticed and thought it was the wind, so he fussed and swapped places with me, and I glanced again at his handsome face. There was something really familiar about him.

"So how are you feeling now?" He asked "Do you feel ready for a hot drink yet?" I nodded, still not feeling completely better, the calmness from the shelter of being on the shore side of the boat was helping. Unexpectedly the sleet had ceased, and some winter sun was peeking out from the thick cloud above us. Within a few minutes he had returned with a hot chocolate for me, and as I sipped it worked its magic and my stomach ached less. The boat had finally levelled off and I felt better.

"Thanks for looking out for me there." I said. "That was really kind of you. You obviously have sea legs." As I said it I couldn't help glancing down to his very long, jean encased muscular legs. I really hoped I hadn't looked either desperate or creepy. He seemed oblivious and laughed showing me his big white teeth. His eyes crinkled up and I knew he was a man who laughed a lot. I could feel myself grinning back at him and hoped that my teeth weren't now covered with chocolate. I definitely felt brighter.

"Where are you heading?" I asked and then realised was a stupid question that was after all we were on a boat with only one destination. "Sorry I meant you don't sound Scottish or Irish I was wondering if you were a tourist. I can't place your accent..." I broke off sheepishly, silently cursing myself. None of this conversation was going to impress him at all. I so needed to improve my chat up lines. I could feel my friends laughing at my inane attempts to keep a conversation going with an attractive man, and one who smelled so delicious as well.

He laughed again, nodding in agreement with me, our arms touching as we leaned over the railing, clutching our drinks, mirroring each other, our bodies in synch.

"Would you believe I'm from Glasgow originally? My family moved to Canada when I was in school, and then I've travelled around a lot since then."

"Oh, that explains it. I'm usually good with accents." I could have slapped myself, where were the angels of conversation when they were needed?

"You seem ok on board the boat do you travel like this often?" Seriously I was going to throw myself overboard. This was pathetic. *Please take pity on a girl who can't flirt.* I prayed silently.

His eyes sparkled again, turning around to lean close to me, partly to make room for other people who had found their way to the sheltered deck.

"I'm a marine biologist." He explained "So I've been on boats for years. Honestly sea sickness can hit you anytime. Even the most experienced sailors can get it without warning."

He had seen me vomit, obviously. I wanted to jump overboard.

"And it always helps to take seasickness pills before going on board." He laughed nudging me in the side and opening his hand to show a packet of dissolve in the mouth seasickness pills.

"I was so impressed there." I laughed as well, gladly popping one of the pills from its plastic blister packaging. He then rolled up his sleeves, a brave thing to do in the still freezing temperature.

"Travel bands work too!" He slipped off a glove, and then expertly took one off and fastened it around my wrist where it nestled against my acupuncture point. I think that was how they were supposed to work.

'I'm now less impressed" and it was my turn to laugh at the same time pulling a face so he knew I was kidding. He was really kind, and we stood in companionable silence for a few minutes.

"So why is a marine biologist on a ferry from Scotland to Ireland?" I asked and as I did so, I felt a little tugging inside of my brain. Something was trying to get my attention, and for the first time I knew that this was significant.

He laughed, shaking his head "Boring work, honestly it's not that interesting."

"Try me." I was still laughing. There was something fun and playful about his good natured teasing. I liked that he didn't try to impress me.

"I was in Scotland monitoring some marine life for my employer and took the opportunity to visit Glasgow to meet some relatives I hadn't seen in a long time."

I waited for him to continue,

"And then I heard that all the flights north of Belfast were cancelled until further notice so I'm heading to the port where I'm catching a boat to take me north to do some more monitoring."

A vision of Grizelle popped into my head and I tried to remember what she said about the whales.

"What are you monitoring?" I asked trying to be casual.

"Well I'm specialising in whale behaviour."

"Are you looking at anything in particular?"

He glanced at me quickly. "We have devised a new sonar technology. I'm assessing its impact on marine life."

I nodded this is exactly what Grizelle was saying to me when we last met.

"Is that the sonar technology some say is responsible for whales beaching all over the British Isles?" I asked with a quick glance at him. He straightened up and I saw a shadow of something flit across his face.

"I'm passionate about marine life." He said "If I thought for one minute there was an issue. I'd pull the plug on the whole experiment. I suppose that's why I'm here. With my background I need to investigate further." He looked back at me.

"What about you?"

"Mmm?" I would never have made a good spy. I was already distracted by both what he said and by his lovely sparkling blue eyes, and that scent was delicious. I turned to look at him again,

"Honestly? I suppose I'm trying to be home for the holidays." He nodded again, as if he understood. His eyes glinted as he screwed them up against an unexpected shaft of weak winter sunshine.

"Where is that?"

"It probably sounds mad." I paused. He was still look-ing at me intently, nodding and his eyes still sparkled. Was that a hint of green in them or a reflection of the dark sea I wondered?

"Well I'm heading to a small town in Ireland to try and meet my dad. I haven't seen him in years, and I suppose I'd like to try and find him soon."

He was looking at me really intently then.

"Where in Ireland are you headed? I'm guessing you would have preferred to fly like every other sane person? This volcanic eruption is crazy isn't it? Who would have expected such a force of nature to have such impact on all of us just trying to get back home or to work?"

I nodded in agreement, and noticed that the sleet had lessened a bit, and the sun was forcing its way through to us. A low mist hung across the water.

"It's a place called Drogheda, you probably never heard of it...." I trailed off.

"No way!" He jumped up, pulling his woollen hat off and running his hands through dark curls, greying slightly at the temples. He'd had a recent haircut and I could see the whiter skin close to his hairline. He pulled his hat back on quickly, in spite of the sun it was still really cold. I couldn't resist raising an eyebrow wondering about his reaction.

"That's where my family is from. We're supposed to be descended from one of the great Irish kings. At least that's what my grandmother used to tell me. Although I bet everyone says that. I haven't been back to Drogheda for years. Gran passed away a couple of years back." I felt a contraction of my heart at that moment. He noticed the corresponding shadow which flicked across my face.

"My gran passed away a couple of weeks ago." I whispered as way of an explanation. I glanced away quickly as I blinked back a tear before I looked back at him. He put his gloved hand on my arm and I knew he got it. He didn't have to say a word, just guided me around so that I was looking out to the sea and the air and the sky. I took some deep breaths.

"So now I'm heading over to Ireland to find my dad so I'm not alone for the holidays." My voice wobbled and I realised that for once in my life I wasn't putting a brave face on things. I wasn't trying to be anyone else. I wanted to be me.

Before I had a chance to say anything else I was aware that there was a roar from the crowd around us. In particular I could hear the shrieks and feel the excitement of young voices. Some children standing near me were screaming,

"Look mammy, look."

And following their outstretched fingers I could see bobbing around on the waves, seals, lots and lots of seals. They dived up and down, in and out of the coal black sea, so close to the boat we could have leaned over and touched them. People around strained to make out the little dog like faces breaking the waves. There must have been a hundred or so, all facing towards us as if we were their entertainment rather than us being theirs.

Within a few minutes another call went out from the people on deck, and we all rushed to look towards the other side of the boat. The roll of the ferry had calmed now, even the sleet had stalled and instead the sea was unexpectedly tranquil. My sea sickness had disappeared completely and with the others I could see a whole group of porpoise breaking the surface, keeping step with the ship before they eventually overtook it. In a formation they swam around and then ahead of us.

I had never seen anything like it, their oily skin glistening in the weak sunshine, almost as dark as the sea all around them. Pushing through and for a moment flying through the foam before descending again beneath. All around me people smiled and laughed with strangers in the unexpected winter sunshine, forgetting the earlier misery of the journey. Above me seabirds flew over and we could hear the noise of their calls even above the noise of the engines. Looking up they too were in a formation, hundreds and hundreds of birds flying like an arrowhead. Some broke off to swoop down and around before flying back to the bigger group. From every direction more and more birds flew into join the group.

The intercom system squealed into life and the tinny sound of the Captain's voice directed us to look to either side of the boat for this very surprising entertainment on the journey. In spite of the cold, I found myself smiling and my travel companion knelt down and was telling the smallest of the children all the details about the seals and porpoise that still surrounded our boat. The engines slowed and stopped as if the Captain had decided that this was something not to be missed. As he did so a strange calm came aboard and all we could hear was the sound of the sea slapping against the boat and the birds above our heads. It was completely quiet without the noise of the engines.

Again, there was another cry of excitement from someone behind me and in the distance away beyond the seals, rapidly heading towards us came flashes of dark and white cutting through the water. Dolphins. All sizes, mummies, daddies and babies. Dancing across the waves, in and out of the seals, cutting through the porpoise. This was a sight like no other. We were all silent, watching, each of us enraptured with the life from the sea. People hugged the rails, each window from the saloons and restaurants full of faces. Smiling at the sea, smiling at each other.

The dolphins laughed and played, each of us on board choosing one or two to track their progress as they swam in and out of the water. At once up on their tails, swimming around each other, like well drilled dancers, and then on their own again. And always as if they too were laughing with us. They connected with us, eyes sparkling, smiling their big grins, mouths stretched in greeting, like us on board. The children laughed and applauded and everyone joined with them. No one could have been unmoved. The Captain's voice cut across us all

"Boys and Girls, Ladies and Gentleman, that was a first for all of us on this deck, and a sight I doubt I will ever see again. I think we have been blessed by Neptune on this voyage."

People smiled and laughed some more, and again another shout was heard way above the noise of joy from the decks.

"Whales!! Look! Look!"

"Did he say whales?" I mouthed at my travel companion, still bent down talking to the kids.

I swear the whole boat rocked not by the wind or sea this time, but by the sheer force of humanity as we all rushed forward to see away in the distance, and again heading quickly towards us, spray on the water. To be more accurate it was actually spraying water like the fire service had set up huge hoses somewhere offshore. At first, I thought it was a play of the wind on the sea until quickly and silently we were aware of these huge water beasts coming closer and closer.

I don't know how many there were. I saw at least six, all of different sizes, babies, young smaller whales, and then huge ones. Easily the size of a bus. I had no idea they were so big or so gentle as the nudged the smaller ones towards us like they were coming to visit family.

I could hear some people around me crying, sniffles from even the biggest men stood there in their winter coats and mufflers. A calm came all over us. Even the children were affected by it. We all stood, one life form truly appreciating another. The whales surrounded the boat and with the seals, porpoise, dolphins and above our heads, the sea birds, we headed across the sea slowly, quietly and in perfect formation. It was the most beautiful moving sight I'd ever been part of.

The engine came on again at a much slower speed, and as the sunshine moved into dusk and the lights of Ireland appeared ahead of us, our marine friends slipped away. As if they had guided us all to safety, and I wondered, me homewards.

As the darkness encroached our boat a final shout came from behind me, and I realised that people were looking up in wonder. The sky was lit up in colour. Greens and blues and yellows all blending into each other. As if the heavens wanted to show us their magic as had the sea. The northern lights, the aurora borealis. I felt so overwhelmed and lucky. And as quickly as it appeared, it too faded away. The journey had been magical. And as a recorded announcement about disembarkation came over the intercom and people started to pull belongings and travelling companions together, I glanced again at the sky and saw that now very familiar symbol lit up in the stars. Archangel Michael watching over me. I looked over to the tall handsome stranger. He was laughing, surrounded by small children and grateful parents. Our eyes met and he smiled, quickly re-joining me as I stood slowly following the crowd as we worked our way down the stairs and through the ferry.

"Thanks again for the journey, and the hot chocolate." I said feeling strangely shy. I mean what you can say in these circumstances. We'd shared an amazing experience and he was heading off to the North Pole or something. I couldn't help myself. I had to say something about the whales.

"After seeing that." I gestured behind me to try to encompass all that we had shared, "How could anyone experiment with marine life? Do you think the whales are being driven ashore because of the American naval experiments? Do you think it's causing any other damage?"

He shook his head, "I don't know, that's what I've been monitoring."

I knew it, for some reason I needed to hear him say it. "Is there nothing you can do?"

"I'm not sure...." It was a question, a gesture perhaps a cop out. I really didn't know. I took a deep breath, blowing it out slowly. I was holding him responsible for something so much bigger and I realised that I was being unfair.

"It was an amazing experience wasn't it?" I whispered.

"The best of my life." He replied, smiling into my eyes and I had a feeling he wasn't only talking about the sea. We smiled again, and as we reached the exit and picked up our bags from the luggage carousel, he leaned over to hug me goodbye. It was brief, and again that fragrance engulfed me.

"I don't even know your name." He whispered.

"I'm Kirsty" I said "Kirsty from Lanark." As he pulled away from me he laughed again.

"So pleased to meet you Kirsty from Lanark. I'm Guy. Guy from Glasgow I guess!" And with that he was gone walking quickly towards a waiting car, US naval flags flying at its corners.

Chapter Twelve

He was gone. The loveliest guy I'd seen in ages had walked out of my life and we hadn't even swapped numbers. He hadn't asked for mine and I was crushed. I'd really thought we'd connected, and then I realised. A guy from Glasgow, just like J.J. had said. She'd been wrong there wasn't a romance, well maybe a romantic moment, yet not what I'd expected. The fortune teller had got it wrong. He wasn't interested in me at all.

As I turned towards the city bus, idling at the kerbside spitting out dark smoke, I felt into my pockets for my gloves. My fingers brushed against something, a card. It burned against my fingers. I know I'd emptied my pockets earlier. They were always full of old bus and train tickets and paper handkerchiefs and I knew they had been empty. It's hard to describe. I had a nice warm feeling inside. This was definitely significant. I jumped into an empty seat, bags squeezed in beside me and in the orangey overhead flickering light I pulled out a postcard from the boat. On the picture side was a seal. On the other was a message, written quickly in capital letters, one letter pushing onto the next in a hurry to get to the point.

Hi, as I write this you've been sick and I'm sure not up to a random stranger asking you out. I'm based in Canada and travel a lot. My name is Guy, incidentally, and lovely to meet you. I hope this isn't creepy (too creepy) I sincerely hope that we can talk and meet at a better time!

He ended it with his email and mobile phone number. I was ecstatic, and could have squealed with joy. He must have written it when he went off to get the drinks even before we started speaking properly. How could he even have thought it was remotely creepy? It was undoubtedly the most romantic thing anyone had ever done. I had a warm feeling all through me. And I sat huddled into my coat, grinning like the proverbial cat that got the cream.

Without delay I pulled out my phone and quickly typed a message and pressed send before any of my usual doubts hit me.

Thank you for the postcard! It will remind me of the best day of my life! It was lovely to meet you. Thanks again for the hot chocolate and for looking after me so well. It would be great to catch up with you sometime. Hope the trip goes well. Kirsty from Lanark!

My friends would be proud of me I thought. Wait until I told them what I'd done. Possibly too many exclamation marks in such a short message the ever present inner critic whispered, but what the hell. He was lovely and he liked me enough to want to keep in touch. As the bus pulled up at the train station I was still grinning as I climbed down. The sleet that had followed me across the sea went unnoticed. Inside the modern styled entrance way, I headed along a corridor to the ticket office and find a way to Drogheda. Excitement made me move quickly, it had been a great day so far and I felt optimistic for the first time in ages.

The ticket office was closed. A very friendly guard came over to me and said he could sell me a ticket and that the next train to Drogheda was due in fifteen minutes. It was so good to hear the lilting Irish accent again. There was something so very comforting about it. People sounded as if they were joking all the time. My heart swelled. It did feel like home. He asked me where I was staying in Drogheda, and I realised I'd forgotten to book anywhere. I'd meant to investigate on the ferry or at the tourist information point at the port. My flirting with Guy had interrupted my great planning. Looking around me in the dark winter I felt a bit foolish. The guard read my mind and laughed in that Irish way I loved,

"Ach don't be worrying about that." He said "Sure my father's second cousin Peggy runs a beautiful wee guest house right at the water's edge, on Hand Street. You can't miss it. Let me give her a ring and see if she can fit you in, and while I do that you have time to grab a coffee from the café over there." And he gestured behind me to the inviting station coffee shop.

As it was I had time to visit the ladies and grab a take-away coffee and pastry before the train arrived. And the guard was as good as his word as he slipped me a note with the address and directions for Mrs Lilly's Guest House in Drogheda. I boarded the train and found an empty carriage and within a few minutes I'd found a seat facing forward and settled back for the journey. I waved at the guard as the train left the bright lights of the station behind us as if he as an old friend. The carriage was empty and I soon gave into the warmth and quiet and dozed off, no doubt drooling as I leaned against the window. The dark fields of Northern Ireland passing by yards away. I woke up with a start a few times as the main towns of the North passed us by. Waking as we headed into Newry, and buying a tea and biscuit from the trolley service. Excitement and nerves filled me as I knew the next stop would be Drogheda.

Would I find my dad? Would he know I was on my way to him? Or was all this a wasted journey?

I'd soon find out.

The train pulled slowly into Drogheda station and for a moment I had a real sense of deja vu. I had been here before. I knew it. As I pulled my bag to climb down from the train a little white feather flew down beside me. It had to be a sign. I had a good feeling. In the dazzle of the brightly lit station I walked along knowing that outside I'd find a car park, and taxi rank. I headed out to the drizzle and noticed the frosted ground, the empty taxi rank and the single car parked at the kerbside. Standing holding a sign with my first name on it was the big white haired man from the ferry. The one who had stopped me falling and told me about Neptune. He was still wearing his waterproof yellow coat. He winked as he saw me.

"Well hello lassie" he said "If I'd known you were coming to stay with us I'd have driven you down with me, save you getting the train. Then again you were probably more comfortable on the train. My van stinks of fish." He laughed and winked again. "Let's get you back to the guesthouse. My wife is dying to meet you again."

With that he gestured towards a small white car.

"Don't worry it's the wife's." He laughed and winked. "She keeps it clean."

I smiled my thanks and settled into the passenger seat, distracted by fixing my seat belt and pushing my bag at my feet. I didn't know where to start. *How was this for a sign? A sign with my name on it.* I couldn't help smile to myself.

In the end I didn't need to ask a single question, Bobby talked from the moment he switched on the engine until five minutes later when he stopped and parked outside a terraced cottage. A lovely looking blonde haired woman was standing on the step waiting for me. I already knew this was his wife, Peggy. That the cottage had six bedrooms, which her father had extended it with his own hands years ago for his ten children, and that Peggy ran it as a bed and breakfast. They'd been married thirty years, had met on the boat to Scotland. He was Scottish, and was semi-retired so did an occasional shift on the boat. What he didn't tell me was how she knew me, he wanted to leave that to his wife to tell all.

As it was, the house was so tiny from the outside I thought he was pitching me a bit of a story. The neat two storey building and bright red painted door opened into a warm front room, with the kitchen out back. As soon as I was guided through, I knew to turn right and go up a little landing to find a narrow staircase to a higher level. There I was shown into a lovely room with a view over the port area, or so she told me, as I couldn't see a thing as night had descended. A memory tugged at my mind.

Had I been here before or did it remind me of a similar place? It was so dark outside that the window was a mirror and all I saw was my own pale faced reflection. I realised that both Peggy and Bobby liked to chat. I hadn't said much more than hello yet knew that she had cooked my favourite potato pie and soda bread and it would be on the table in five minutes.

I didn't even know I had a favourite. This was going to be interesting if a little unsettling. Perhaps she was mixing me up with someone else. They both seemed really kind and sincere and I didn't have any strange feelings, so I quickly washed my hands and face in the en-suite bathroom. Hot water and gorgeous rose scented soap did the trick to wake me up. I struggled to pull a brush through my tangled hair given the wind and rain had attacked it on the voyage, so pulled it into a messy bun then retraced my steps downstairs and into the lounge. A roaring peat fire welcome me, and dinner was out on the table. She had set it with a lovely crisp well ironed Irish linen cloth, my gran had similar so now I guessed I knew where she'd got them. There were huge platters of food easily enough to feed a dozen people. We had potato pie, soda bread, and heaps of vegetables. Everything steamed away, melted butter on top, glistened in the overhead light. My mouth watered and stomach growled. I was starving.

Peggy shovelled out huge portions talking at the same time about recipes, growing vegetables, favourite foods, Scotland, Ireland, visitors, running a B and B. She provided a running commentary all the time her husband and I sat eating. I didn't think she'd ever stop. No wonder he had chatted so much in the car, it was probably the only time he got the chance. She sipped some tea but didn't eat anything, so there was no halt in the conversation when I could ask a question. I just hoped she'd eventually tell me what I wanted to know.

"So Kirsty, do you remember the pie? You loved it when you were a child. I think the last time you stayed here you were about eight or nine. Do you remember it? You and your daddy came over for a few days. I think your mammy wasn't very well at the time." She crossed herself and looked heavenwards at that moment so I knew she had heard that my mum had died. I realised that there was a huge part of my life that other people knew more about than I did. This was going to be very interesting and illuminating. The question was would she tell me what I wanted to know, or would I ever get a minute to ask her.

There seemed to be a tiny lull in the conversation as she took a longer than normal sip of her tea. It might have been the mention of my mum and her attempt to be respectful to that.

"Mrs Lilly."

"Please call me Peggy, Kirsty"

"Okay, sorry Peggy."

"Oh Bobby listen to that lovely accent. I just love a Scottish accent. It takes me back. I think you've lost yours you know." She interrupted and I wondered if I'd ever get the chance to talk. A huge portion of apple pie and double cream was plopped in front of me. The steam rose to meet my twitching nose. The moment was lost and she continued.

"We are all delighted that you've come home Kirsty. It's been too long. Your grandfather can't wait to see you. He knew you'd come. Didn't he Bobby. He said that last week didn't he? Wait til Kirsty gets here he said. Didn't he Bobby?" She nodded over at her husband who winked again at me.

I heard nothing else she said for a few minutes from the ringing in my ears. I actually thought I would faint I got such a fright.

"My grandfather?! I whispered. "My grandfather?" She stopped talking for a moment. Only to then go on.

"Why of course, isn't that why you are here? He said you'd come when you knew what was happening, didn't he Bobby?"

She kept talking. I was somewhere else, physically sitting there in her front room, but my mind minutes behind, still trying to process the bombshell. I saw her mouth move but I heard nothing else.

I said again "My grandfather?"

With a nod, Bobby started clearing plates and gestured over to the fire place. He could sense I was in shock, even if Peggy had too much to tell me to register my pale face and whispered repetition. He passed me a mug of tea that I hugged to my chest for comfort.

"Can you tell me where he is?" I whispered again. It worked and she heard me. "Billy? Where he always is."

I felt a bit foolish then. "Where is that?"

She looked at me a bit strangely as if she was becoming aware that I was a bit slow on the uptake.

"Newgrange." Bobby said. "At the house. Do you remember it?"

Newgrange again. That place I thought I'd never known. From my expression he knew that I didn't remember, and something passed between them both. A little look of some kind. I didn't know what it meant.

"Kirsty we thought you'd come to help with.... well with the trouble. The way your family does. Your grandfather he hasn't been very well. He kept saying that you would be on your way. I know your dad called you as well."

"How did you know that?" I asked "How do you know my dad? Is he here? I came to find him." I looked pleadingly from one kind face to another. "I wanted to find him." How could I tell them that I hadn't even considered having a grandfather as well?

"Is there any other family here?" I asked, embarrassed.

"You're related to most of Drogheda, and probably have of the country Kirsty! I'm related to you through your grandmother Molly. Sadly she passed away when your dad was a boy. Billy and Molly Fey were an amazing couple. Always helping people out. You've got the look of her so you have, I think it's your colouring."

"People always say I look like my mum and her mother." I answered as if it really mattered. Blood was blood. I came to find my dad and had found another relative I had forgotten. How shallow would that sound to people? How quickly we can leave people behind. I felt ashamed of myself.

"I was called Wallace after my mother's side."

"Aye, that was a strange one for us all here. We knew it was important to your mum and grandmother, but we always think of you as a Fey, after your dad's family."

I nodded at the pair as if I understood decisions made by my parents all those years ago. They both seemed subdued for a moment, lost in their own memories no doubt.

"Is there any way to get to see my grandfather tonight?" I asked. The reproduction Swiss clock on the wall ticked loudly, and on the hour, a little plastic drummer boy soldier popped out. We waited until he finished hitting his drum for the count of seven, then the door closed as he popped back inside.

"It's much too late to visit him now" said Bobby, "we usually go on a Sunday afternoon when it's easier for his visitors. Tomorrow afternoon is probably best. I'll call and let him know you are coming. He'll be so excited to see you."

"Thank you. Is there any news on where my dad might be? He phoned me from this number two weeks ago, and I've rung it every day since, no one answered." I showed them the number I'd found out when I press redial that day in Angel's Cakes after he'd called me. I'd saved into my mobile phone and had dialled it hundreds of times over the last couple of weeks. Hoping that he'd answer me.

"That's the telephone number of the Newgrange visitor centre" said Peggy "I volunteer there. It's been flooded so no one has been in for the last couple of weeks. Your dad was doing some of his work there. That must be why he phoned you."

"His work Peggy? What "work"? What was he doing there?" I looked from one concerned face to the other.

"He said that the stones were in danger. What do you think he meant? Do you know what has happened and why he said he needed me?" I realised that my voice was shaking. I so badly needed them to understand how much this meant to me. "Is he still there?"

Peggy nodded her head, her eyes full of concern for me. I knew she was trying to help and she probably didn't have a clue what was happening. How could she when I didn't know either? Sitting there by the peat fire, warm and full from all the delicious food I wanted nothing more than to close my eyes and wake up in a happy home, with family all around me. It was, I realised my dream, and yet a little sensation inside me warned that wasn't likely to happen. I had a feeling that something was about to change. I didn't know what, all I could do was keep moving and let it find me. Whatever that was. The older lady leaned closer to me, I could smell the hairspray she used mixed with the smell of peat from the fire.

"I told you it's been closed. The river flooded and the building is damaged. We're waiting for it to dry out before it opens again. Your dad was there last time I was there. You know what he's like. He's always on the move, doing what he does."

Bobby flicked on the television, and the loud sound of the news filled the room. I jumped at the volume and thought perhaps he had done it to break the conversation up. He turned it down to a more comfortable level with an apologetic wink, as his wife started talking again about all the terrible news in the world, and everything she had read in the last month's newspapers. Sitting at the edge of their pale green velour sofa, realising that possibly everything I needed to know was in this couple's memories and minds was incredibly frustrating. I had no idea how to get it from them without resorting to torture. This would be a lesson in patience for me.

Bobby interrupted my thoughts.

"Would you look at that, it's a disgrace so it is." We all turned towards the screen, and there in full high definition colour were scenes filmed earlier of a huge whale washed up on a beach. My heart thudded and I felt it hit my stomach. Bobby had been on the boat with me. He had seen that most amazing sight. The majesty of the seas. We'd both witnessed it together. I looked at him and could see he was as moved as I was. He sat shaking his head, his disbelief and shock mirroring my own. Peggy was oblivious to the effect it was having on us. In her own way she was upset. It could have been one of our beautiful whales lying on its side, dead and bloated and now an inconvenience to the authorities who would have to dispose of it. I felt sick.

Bobby turned up the volume a little and we heard the newscaster telling us that the whale had beached itself at Bettystown beach. Bobby mouthed that was only a mile or so away from where we sat. It had to have been one of the pod we'd watched only a couple of hours ago. He continued to shake his head, tears were in our eyes.

"So pointless, how could that have happened?" Bobby told Peggy our experience on board ship when we were witnessed to the marvels of the sea, and then he miserably motioned towards the screen where a reporter was standing with his back to this huge carcass. He said that the beaching was unexplained and was the tenth on the coast in the last twelve months. I raised an eyebrow to Bobby at that, and he nodded in agreement. So many and all unexpected.

"Would you look at that" he shouted out.

"We're on the news." He pointed at the screen which showed a helicopter light illuminating some water and what looked like a port area. His eyes were sharper than me and he had immediately recognised Drogheda. The weird thing was at that very same time we heard the sound of a helicopter swooping low overhead lighting up the front and then the back of the house. He swore in shock and both of them ran out towards the back garden, me following behind. The helicopter had conveniently lit up the scene down below at the port side. Its blades powering over our heads, blasting away at the garden. Television forgotten, we stood up on tip toe to get a better look. It was difficult to tell what was happening. It looked like a rescue of some sort. People, emergency lighting, blue flashing lights from the Garda police force. The rich roast of burning peat, smoke from chimneys gathered with the mist, the light from the search lights catching smoke fragments in the air, and far in the distance I saw the lights of a train going over the metal railway bridge which spanned the port area.

As exciting as it was I suddenly had an overwhelming need to join whatever was happening at the port. I didn't know what I would find but something made me grab my coat, hat and gloves and rush out to the sound of the helicopter above my head and Peggy and Bobby calling after me to be careful. I'd gone beyond that. All I knew was that there was something at the port side I needed to see.

Chapter Thirteen

The light and sound from the hovering helicopter acted as a beacon to me and I followed it down to the port. Running quickly through the dark streets it only took a few minutes for me to reach the search lights and the large group of people milling around. I squeezed through the crowd, stopping to try to get my bearings. Looking up and to my left I saw the rail bridge that spanned the river Boyne. Buildings on either side of the river must have been warehouses and there were some rusting old boats tied up.

As I got closer to the front, from the search lights I could see that there were some rubber dinghies in the water. The fluorescent strips across their hulls caught the light to show that they were police launches, with male and female officers in wet suits and diving gear on board. At the edge of the concrete port and just slightly out of my vision was where everyone was concentrated. People dressed in brightly coloured waterproof jackets clustered and seemed to be leaning over the edge focusing on something in the water. From the conversations and chat I overheard I realised that a couple of them were veterinarians. There had to be an animal in distress.

I felt compelled, forced even to push forward. I needed to see what was happening. As I leaned further over the side, the light glistened on the surface, an oily blackness and I knew what it was. Banging against the port wall, lifeless, with its eyes closed was a baby whale. I was sure it was one that we'd seen earlier today.

Tears sprung to my eyes, I could hardly breathe as my hands covered my mouth to stop me calling out. It seemed so unfair. So awful that I was so close to such a beautiful animal. One by one, the rescue party pulled away from the body. I realised that the vets had stethoscopes and had been frantically trying to find a heartbeat. The Garda in the boats were using buckets and bottles to pour water onto the animal under guidance from the vets who seemed to be in control, and the other people standing around were like me. Unable to do a thing except pray.

The sleet fell all around us as I looked onto the icy black river. The sky above dark and without a star in sight. Scarcely able to believe that another beautiful whale was dying in front of us. I could hear people discussing how it had got so far upstream, almost into the heart of the city. Those who had like me, seen the news, talked about the whale beaching at the nearby beach.

I don't know what came over me there standing on the port side at Drogheda. Perhaps it was just the sadness and unfairness of it all. Perhaps I felt I needed to give something in return for the beautiful experience I'd had on the boat. I just knew I couldn't walk away. I knew I had to do something to save this beautiful sea beast.

I pushed through to the front.

The two vets were shaking their heads, signalling to the Garda to pull back their boats that I then realised were propping up the baby whale's body.

"You can't stop!" I shouted above the noise of the heli-copter above us, its blades whipping the choppy waters of the Boyne. The wining drone of the outboard motors of the support boats bounced off the walls of the port buildings.

"There's nothing else we can do miss." Said the taller of the two men. I could see he looked exhausted, and both were shivering uncontrollably.

"We've been trying for an hour. This wee fella has gone. He's exhausted and in shock. There's nothing that we can do. It would take a miracle to save him."

"He shouldn't be here." His younger colleague added. "He must have got separated from his family and he's lost and too exhausted to get back out to sea. The tide has turned and there's nothing that can be done."

Something changed for me that night. I still don't know what happened. All I remember is that I lay down on the port wall, the icy stone instantly freezing me, in spite of my warm down filled coat. I felt like something was beneath the stones reaching up to me. Pulling me down. Quickly ripping off my gloves, I stretched out and managed to reach the body of the whale. Tears ran down my face as my bare outstretched fingertips made contact. I was oblivious to the sleet, the ice, the darkness and the sounds all around me. Everything faded away and I felt that it was just me and my lovely memories of that morning. I could see again the whales as they surrounded the boat and seemed to guide us into Belfast. I must have cried and cried as I remembered what a beautiful experience that had been. As I lay there I could sense a heartbeat. It seemed to come from below me as if the earth was sending out a message to me or through me, I wasn't aware fully of what I was attempting or why.

I had no idea at the time, all around me others too lay down and touched the baby whale. At least six other people joined me, and as we did that, a couple of the police divers also jumped into the icy river and laid their hands on it too.

As I lay there, wet and freezing to the core I felt a flutter under my fingers. It happened again. I opened my eyes to find there were at least a dozen other hands joining me. As I looked from one to another, we all wore the same determined look on our faces. We were not giving up.

The baby whale flicked its tail. Its eyes opened and it gave another shake and shudder of its body. I let go, and struggled to my knees, hampered by and suddenly aware of the weight of my coat. Taking my lead the others let go as well. With only a quick glance in our direction the baby whale pushed away from the old stone wall.

It swam off, dropping under the surface for only a moment, before resurfacing and swimming off away from us towards the sea. We were frozen, wet and euphoric. The vets, the Garda and other bystanders all shaking their heads in amazement. Away in the distance, beyond the rail bridge, the helicopter picked up the glistening bodies of three other whales. The baby headed towards them.

The people on the port erupted in noisy congratulations. Hugging each other, many people were crying, slapping each other on the back. I was still kneeling on the ground. Stunned but satisfied. Something came into my mind. A feeling of strength. I'd never felt like that before. My legs felt stronger, solid, like I was rooted into the ground. This place felt like home. With that I left the harbour behind me and headed back to Hand Street. Guided by an old familiarity, I walked the ancient streets, detouring past the

Magdelene Tower and St Laurence Gate. I stopped there for a moment. I could feel it. The old stones felt alive to me. Something had shifted and for the first time ever I felt strong as if I too was made of stone. Like I was as old as the earth itself. It didn't make any sense to me.

Chapter Fourteen

It took me ages to warm up back at Hand Street. After making a really big fuss of me, and some hot chocolate, Peggy and Bobby eventually left me alone. It seemed my escapades had been caught on camera, and the phone hadn't stopped ringing. I should have realised that everyone in Drogheda and I suppose in other parts of Ireland would have known that I was staying at Peggy's place. She seemed to know everybody. I learned that we were related as my maternal grandmother was her father's second cousin or some kind of connection.

I was exhausted and excused myself so that I could get to bed, yet it took me ages to sleep. My head was buzzing with the feelings I now had. Peggy had filled me in that my father's family had been known as healers, so she wasn't surprised that I'd put my hands on the baby whale to such a positive effect. If she'd told me that at supper I don't suppose I would have believed her, afterwards I had to admit that something really special had happened. Perhaps that had been the connection between my parents that I hadn't even known about. Both coming from long lines of healers. It made sense, if any of the last few weeks could, and I suppose what rattled around in my head was *what did that mean for me?*

The feeling I'd had as I pushed through to the quay side was unlike anything I'd ever known before. I did it without thinking and I had needed to hold out my hands to the whale, and then afterwards I'd felt so strong, and I suppose *connected* in a way I'd never experienced before. Something strange was happening to me.

I eventually fell into a dreamless sleep, waking just after six am in the darkness, and then slept again. This time I dreamt that the old man I'd met at the Druid's temple met me at another set of stones. This time they were heaped on top of each other, they kept shaking and falling down to roll down a hillside, he asked me to lift them back to the top. Then the earth would shake and the stones would roll again down to the bottom of the hillside once more. He took me to a small house inside the stones, he made me tea and showed me a photo album full of photographs of me as a child, then the house shook and the roof fell off and rolled down the hill again. This happened again and again until I woke up with a fright, not knowing where I was for a few minutes, except that I had urgent business to attend to. It really was the scariest feeling, my heart thumped, and the hair at the nape of my neck was damp.

I heard a knocking at the door, and Peggy calling my name brought me back to earth. She said she had breakfast almost out and wanted to give me some notice so I could get ready first. I was extremely grateful for her intervention, and threw back the duvet. Quickly showering in the little bathroom which was painted a pretty pale blue with sea shells dotted around it in a nautical theme. The towels were thick and soft and navy blue with a white and pink trim. I dried my hair with a hairdryer set up at a small white vanity table at the window and from there I could see down to the quayside. Weak sunshine tried to peak through a cloudy sky and when it did it bounced off the dark water beneath me. I still felt strange.

Peggy called my name again and I reluctantly left the view behind to walk downstairs where I was met with another huge feast. Toast, cereal, eggs, potato cakes, butter, jam, and a pot of tea. All sitting waiting for me and again the table set with a beautiful linen and lace trimmed cloth. She smiled and gave me a hug.

"It is so grand to see you Kirsty. Thank you for what you did last night. Since I've had you in the house I've had a really good feeling. I know things are going to work out. We've got no need to worry about anything."

"What do you mean Peggy?" I asked. "What would you be worrying about? Is this something to do with my dad?"

"Have your breakfast first, then we'll sort out our day." Her phone rang and she smiled an apology as she went off to answer it.

"Bobby has been called up to the ferry again this morning, so he won't be back until late." She called over her shoulder.

Breakfast was delicious, exactly what I needed. I heard her talking to someone on the phone for a while, and then her phone rang and again she chatted away. In the meantime I sat looking out the window, watching Drogheda life pass me by. I had to admit that there was a familiarity about the view. I day dreamed for a while, the winter sun through the glass warming me. There was a bubble of excitement growing in me at the thought of meeting my grandfather and my father. I really hoped that would work out. I knew a couple of things I didn't know before I came to Drogheda. My grandfather was still alive. My dad must have been called Billy after his father, and my grandmother had been called Molly, and there were healers in my family. All of this was news to me.

Peggy came back into the room to tidy away with breakfast dishes.

"So that's all organised for you." She said. "I've arranged a car to take you to Newgrange this morning. The Centre still isn't open officially, my friend Martha will show you the site, and then you can go to see your grandfather later. I haven't been able to track down your dad yet. Don't worry about that. As soon as he knows you are here he'll find you."

She seemed so sure that I felt I should trust her.

"Why don't you get yourself ready? Martha will be here in ten minutes. I'm sorry I can't take you. You see it's my turn to help out at the church's coffee morning. I can't get anyone to cover for me. Martha is heading over to see her daughter and new baby granddaughter so she's happy to drop you off at Newgrange and I can pick you up later. Here's my number give me a ring and I'll come and get you."

I had time to find my coat, Peggy had dried it off for me, along with my hat, scarf and gloves. I popped my phone into my little black leather rucksack, and checked that my purse was still there. A car horn sounded outside and Peggy shouted up to me that her friend was waiting for me. She gave me a quick hug as I passed her on my way out of the house. There was something about the whole interaction that bothered me yet I was so focused on the tasks in hand so I wasn't late, that I didn't stop to ask what it was.

Martha was waiting for me and gave me a cheery welcome as I climbed into her big four wheel drive truck. She was a very petite red haired lady, and I wondered if she struggled to see over the steering wheel. However, she expertly turned the car around and soon we had left the town behind and were flying along the country lanes past cute pastel painted cottages and lush green fields. Martha explained that there had been lots of flooding but that she could take me into the Newgrange site. The Visitor Centre was still officially closed. No one was there, it would take another few days for the water levels to retract to let the Centre open again. They were all worried because hundreds of people from all over the world were due at the site for the winter solstice celebrations. She told me that every year there was a ballot and that if your name was pulled out you got a ticket to enter Newgrange for the solstice.

"Can you tell me about Newgrange?" I asked. "I don't know much about it, yet I know that my dad wants me to help in some way."

"Newgrange is a really special place, in an area of special places. There are over ninety monuments in the Bru na Boinne, the name given to this area. It means Palace of the Boyne, and it is now a World Heritage Site. There is more megalithic art here than anywhere in Western Europe. Newgrange, and the other passage tombs at Dowth and Knowth are Neolithic or late Stone Age. Yet what is most important to me is that this place is also of spiritual significance as well. Our old legends and folklore connect the ancient kings of Ireland with this place, with the caves and chambers within the site. Your dad was worried about a new vibration he'd sensed in the stones. He was investigating whether sonar technology the Americans are using had affected the stones, so that they were loose and would move. This really scared him, and that there would be a terrible implication for us if the stones moved. He said he'd do whatever it took to stop it happening. That's when he called you."

With that little bombshell she took her eyes from the twisting and turning road and glanced over at me. I was shocked. Like someone had decided to punch my stomach with a fist in a jagged glove. So this is why Peggy had arranged for Martha to drive me. She knew all about my dad and his activities. She knew he'd called me, and most importantly, she also knew why. I should have guessed, and if I'd taken a moment to ask why this morning, all of this wouldn't have been such a shock to me. We could have had a normal conversation, instead it was like I was the last to know, and that really hurt.

The idea that the stones at Newgrange had moved was obviously a fear of my father's that for some reason was transferred into my recent recurring nightmare. That horrible night terror that was waking me up in a panic, of me dying at the back of the stone chamber with people running as they tried to save themselves as the sun failed to light the chamber. Now I'm told that the solstice celebrations might not go ahead due to flooding and also that Dad believed the sonar experiments were causing the stones to vibrate and move. I needed to know more.

"I don't understand how sonar technology would affect the stones? Could it really move stones? How big are they?"

She chanced a glance at me again, this time I caught it and saw her eyes were a rich brown, with little flecks of amber in the iris. I'd seen that colour of eyes before.

"Do I know you Martha?"

She smiled at that.

"I haven't seen you since you were a child. I wondered if you'd recognise me. I'm a cousin of your father. His father Billy was my mother's brother. They were very close, so they were. Like me and your dad were. We've got that kind of family so we have. Everyone says we look like brother and sister. We've definitely got the same eyes."

I was silent for a moment. The idea that she was so close to my father, and obviously knew him so well. For a moment I felt sad that I'd not had that closeness. As much as I'd loved Gran, how different would my life have been if I'd had cousins to play with. She rubbed my arm, and I knew she could sense my sadness.

Whatever was going on here I felt that I had to wait for the information to come to me. Asking the wrong questions wouldn't help right now. I guessed that if I did she wouldn't fill in the blanks for me. Another lesson in patience. A few minutes passed and she didn't add anything about my dad. So he wasn't up for discussion, I had to find out more about the stones. I asked again.

"I don't understand about the sonar technology moving the stones. Is that really possible?"

"Some people, your dad and me included, believe that sound waves were what was used to move and build ancient stone structures. If we could find the correct frequency we could replicate that. So we think the sonar must be close to that particular frequency. After all it's affecting the whales isn't it? It must be some sort of natural frequency, whales are beaching themselves all around the coast line. You know all about that, don't you?"

With that she glanced over again, meeting my eyes and squinting at me. She obviously knew about the rescue last night.

"What's the significance of the stones moving? What do you think would happen? Why does it matter so much?"

And why am I here? I really wanted to know and was afraid to ask.

"Your dad is the clever one in the family. He was the one who went off to university in Glasgow to study archaeology. He was exploring the connections between Ireland and Scotland, like the origins of the Scottish Stone of Destiny. He specialised in pre historic times. He was always so fascinated by Newgrange given the family connection."

"The family connection?"

"Maybe I should leave some things for him to explain."

"Tell me about the Stone of Destiny? It means a lot to us Scots. What do you mean about its origins? Surely it's as Scottish as me?"

She smiled. "How Scottish are you again Kirsty?"

I had to laugh at that. If anyone asked me I'd say half Scottish, and half Irish. *Was that what she meant about the Stone of Destiny? How could that be possible?*

"Your dad will fill you in on his research. He's been looking at its origins, it might have come from Egypt with a princess called Scotia. Did you know that?"

Before I had the chance to ask more she turned away from me and gestured over her shoulder. I'd been so distracted I hadn't realised that we had arrived at the site. I could see an old stone wall and high wooden gate, yet I felt something pull me, a connection of some kind.

"It is five thousand years old, so built before either the pyramids in Egypt or even Stonehenge in England. What you see here today is after the renovations, the interior remains untouched really. Wait until you see it again. Let me get the key for the gate and show you around as much as I can. It's wonderful, do you remember it from when you were a girl?"

I was about to say not really, until as I climbed down from the car and my feet hit the ground, the weirdest sensation came over me. Everything about the place was instantly familiar. The old stone dyke, the gate, the pathway round to the right, and then the greenest of grass covered hill and a view of a white quartz crystal fronted building standing proud at the top. It was beautiful, stunning and I knew it so well. I had been here before, it felt like many times.

How could I ever have forgotten this place? I glanced over at Martha, she smiled back at me, her eyes glowed with brightness and love and pride in showing me the site. As we entered into the fenced off field I realised how high we were, with a perfect view of the valley. Although it was a dull day, occasional shafts of weak sunlight found their way through the grey skies to glint off the white quartz wall. My feet and legs felt like I was walking through a field of static, such a strong connection did I feel with the land. With each foot step it was as if I was going back in time. I felt younger and wanted to run around. I'd not felt like that for a very long time.

We walked up a wide pathway to the top of the hill, where the largest of the site stones lay on its side. It was possibly eight feet wide and covered in carvings of spirals and diamond shapes, like those I knew so well from the marker stones at home, and those I saw at the Druid's temple. I reached out to trace their faint outline with my gloved hands, before pulling off my gloves to feel the stone with my bare fingers. This was so familiar. A childhood memory came to mind. I saw myself running around the grass, chasing about the stones, playing hide and seek with a man who laughed a lot. Dancing around with him, my little feet on his as he guided me in some steps. The sensation of flying through the air as he lifted me up onto his shoulders, then ducking down as we entered the chamber. I felt so very close to my dad at that moment.

Gratefully I smiled at Martha. I could only whisper my thanks, scared I'd start to cry. I so wanted to see my dad. I'd missed him in my life for much too long. A little spasm flicked across my heart. I needed him to be ok.

"Do you want to go inside the tomb?" She asked. "I don't have time today to take you to Dowth or Knowth, but they are not like this. They don't have the same spiritual energy for me. This place is so very special. Do you remember it Kirsty?"

"Oh Martha, yes I do. I'd forgotten all about this place. I used to play here didn't I? Dad was working, measuring stones and doing all sorts of experiments, I think it was geophysical. I remember him wandering around with different equipment. I'd love to go inside again if that's ok. Do you think he is still here, or near here?"

Even as I said it I knew the answer for myself. He wasn't at this place. There was something else, a shadow on the edge of my attention. Something trying to get my notice. I turned away from Martha for a moment, and took a breath and closed my eyes for a second and then I felt it.

I wouldn't see him for some time. I would see him soon. I don't know how I knew it yet I sensed that it was true.

She smiled again and I knew that she knew this already. She held out her hand to guide me over to the chamber within the hillside. I was ready for some answers.

Chapter Fifteen

Some small wooden steps sat at the front of the monument to help us climb up about six feet on to a wooden open slatted bridge. As it was so narrow, we edged across it carefully, me following Martha. There was a deep ditch below us full of boulders so I held tightly to the handrail. At the entrance she tugged back a heavy looking green tarpaulin and pulled out a small pen torch. The entrance was surprisingly small and we had to squeeze sideways down the tight passageway. With each step I felt that feeling of familiarity. I had walked this pathway hundreds of times before. This was the first time I'd done it as an adult, so it was a much cosier fit than I remembered. Martha was smaller than me, and even she had to flatten her jacket and had slung her bag over her shoulder so she wouldn't catch it on the stone walls that lined our path seeming to hold back the hillside. Is that why my dad was so worried? If any of these stones moved even a centimetre would the whole thing come crashing down? As we proceeded along, the dirt beneath my feet was filled with footprints, modern soles. I wondered how many people before that had trodden the same way. It was nearly eighty feet long Martha told me, she was an excellent source of information as she guided her torch around the stones showing me carvings she found significant. Her voice carried back to me in a strange whispery way, sometimes disappearing completely so I had to ask her to repeat what she said. Like the stones didn't want me to hear too much about them.

In this space and place how could anyone doubt that we were connected to the earth and to our ancestors? How had they ever managed to build this five thousand years ago?

My feet scuffed along the earthen floor and I shuddered as I remembered my dream. The same dank, damp odour was there. The stone sides sharp as they snagged my coat and hair. Even so I had a new fascination for this place. I mulled it over in my mind as we walked forward, guided by Martha's torch.

What was its importance, and why was Dad so worried?

Martha stopped suddenly and flashed her tiny light around what must have been the centre of the tomb. There was very little illumination so scary shadows hung everywhere. The sound of our own steps and breathing bouncing off the walls as if we were surrounded by many other people. The walk had taken my breath away and I realised we had been climbing uphill. There was a slight incline built into the chamber. It was clever yet I couldn't help myself from thinking *what lies beneath us?* Ahead of and to our left and right were three circular shaped stone chambers, about eight feet wide and less than that in height. A tall man wouldn't have been able to easily stand up in there. The chambers to my left and right hosted huge shallow stone basins, the stone cut so thin it was almost transparent. They were easily five feet in diameter so I couldn't explain how they could have been carried along the pathway. The monument had to have been built all around them. The chamber ahead of us was bare except for stones and dirt, and the smell of damp and decay.

Martha explained that it was believed that sacrifices were possibly made in the chamber. This didn't seem likely to me, as there was such a lovely feeling in the space, despite the smell. She said that precisely at 8.58am at the winter solstice on 18th December, and over the next five days, a sunbeam would enter the chamber through a slit at the entrance and work its way along the pathway. The beam widened to seventeen centimetres and lit up the darkness of the chamber until hitting upon a spiral carving on the wall of the empty centre chamber ahead of us. The whole event lasted for seventeen minutes exactly, and then the light disappeared. I asked her the significance of the number seventeen, she shrugged and told me my dad would be able to tell me more. She said that the previous year thirty-five thousand people had entered into the ballot to attend, so many wanted to, and only twenty or so per day were lucky.

As she told me this she moved the light back and forth across the dirt floor, ending with the light on the triple spiral stone carving at the head of the chamber. I shivered, the symbol that I'd known all my life. One I'd seen in the stones at home in Scotland, at the Druid temple before I'd come to Ireland, and then I realised with a shake of my head, it was also on the pendant I had been given as a child. No wonder it was so familiar to me. Old symbols surrounded me and I now knew another one for Archangel Michael that Angel had shown me.

What was their significance though?

Martha's mobile phone rang and with it news from her daughter about lunch arrangements, and so the spell I was under was interrupted. It was time to go and leave symbols and old stones behind like I'd done before. As we retraced our steps, Martha started talking about the Irish legends and their connection with the site. She said it was believed that the Giants of Old, the High Kings of Ireland had been buried at Newgrange, also called the Palace of the Boyne which was the river the town of Drogheda had been built on, and which had given the valley its name. She continued on that myths and legends told that there were supernatural beings who had gone to live in fairy hills, and that Newgrange was at the centre of all of that. With the feeling I had at that moment I really could believe it and wondered for a moment if they were still there. Ireland felt like that kind of place to me.

Outside she wanted to point out to me some of the standing stones that she said edged what was called a cursus, a procession route which ran for hundreds of feet across the landscape. I was reminded of the labyrinth the old man at the Druid's Temple had mentioned to me. I asked her did they know what the carvings meant or if they recognised the language.

"Druids we believe."

She could see from my face I was shocked.

"I was just thinking about another Druid's place I know." I answered her questioning expression.

I had an overwhelming urge to touch one of the larger of the stones near the entrance and as I did so I felt a strong heartbeat. Like it was alive. I leaned against it, my head resting there for a moment. There was heat and a light feeling. I could have stayed there all day.

How could anyone not feel this? I thought to myself.

"Martha, at the quayside last night. I felt quite strange. Not like myself at all. Peggy said something about healers in the family. Do you know anything about that? Or can you tell me anything?"

She smiled and pulled her jacket closer around her, for a moment I felt bad about keeping her out in the cold and thought she might not say much to me.

"I feel your Dad will tell you more about that. It's not through his mum's side of the family. It's come through his dad's. Years ago his family were well regarded as spiritual healers. People would arrive from all over the country to the house to see his grandfather. Honestly Kirsty, when I found out what you had done. Laying your hands on that poor animal I had the feeling that you had the gift as well. I am sure that's why your dad wanted you here. You can do so much good, for us all. For the land. I have a really good feeling about it. I feel that if you wait it will all happen. You don't need to rush anything. Let the land work through you." She smiled softy at me, and I knew she was speaking from her heart.

I felt that Martha had indulged me enough and I didn't want to keep her. The day was dry and not too cold, and despite the gloom the view across the fields was incredible and I didn't want to leave, not yet.

"Martha would you mind if I stayed a while? I really feel connected to this place and I don't want to hurry away."

"Not a problem Kirsty, I feel the same way. Let me point out your grandfather's place. It's only about fifteen minutes' walk from here. From there you can call a taxi, catch a bus on the main road, or give Peggy a ring and she'll come and get you. Are you sure that's what you want to do?"

She pointed out a white building at the bottom of the hill, possibly only a mile or so away. I knew it would be an easy walk down towards it.

"Keep to the roadway mind" she said "don't go over the field."

"Why?" I asked. "Is it boggy?"

"Not too bad now" she laughed. "I just don't want the faery folk to dance away with you!"

I joined in her laughter.

What was the chance of that? A little white feather dropped down onto my jacket. We both laughed again. I could see from her face she knew all about angels. She turned and shouted something to me as she climbed into her car.

"Don't go into any of the faery rings Kirsty, or there is every chance the faeries will dance you away, and we'd never see you again! I mean it now!"

She added that I was to slam the gate behind me when I as leaving, and she'd come and lock it properly later on her way home.

I was still laughing at the idea of the faeries as I turned to walk back towards the monument. The white quartz front glistened like snow and ice and I was reminded of Scotland and my friends in Lanark. I wondered how Grizelle was coping on her boat. Thinking of her made me feel closer and I had a feeling that she was fine. Angel's smiling face came into my mind and I knew that she was also happy. She had said that she thought things were starting again. She was so very wrong. I was standing in Ireland at a stunning ancient monument, surrounded by a beautiful energy. The angels were still with me and I was going to meet my grandfather soon, and then hopefully see my dad. What could possibly go wrong?

Chapter Sixteen

H ugging my coat around me I wandered back along the pathway towards the temple. The quartz front took my breath away as it was stunning, glowing in the winter light.

How on earth had they managed to bring in such big cobbles of quartz? How had they built it so it was in perfect alignment with the winter solstice sunrise, and for seventeen minutes exactly? I had so many questions, I really wanted to know more about the archaeology of the place. It was really special, I could feel it.

I seemed to have walked around the cursus Martha had mentioned to me, and was aware that it was spiralling around the hillside. Just like a labyrinth. I wondered if walking around in a spiral could really take you to a different dimension. I shook my head, trying to clear it of the mad thoughts. I was away with the faeries I thought, sniggering to myself. I wanted to know more about it all as it was fascinating. I wondered if I'd ever get a chance to talk to my dad about any of it. As I wandered, my head full of thoughts, I soon found myself on the other side of the hill at the back of the monument. I was so high that I had a 360 degree view. I was aware of the big sky and green fields that went on for miles and miles, even though it was deep in winter. Far in the distance I saw a haze of dark grey which I wondered was the sea. My mind returned to the whales from yesterday. I hoped that they were safe, for the moment anyway. Who knows how long before another sonar would send them off course again. I hoped that there would be someone close to save them. This shouldn't be happening.

As I wandered around, I was drawn to a huge stone. It must have been at least four metres high, and at least twice as wide as me. It was covered in spiral carvings, etched into the surface thousands of years before, and yet still visible on the worn stone. There was a shimmer in the stone so that even though they were the same colour it still sat out against the background of the pale grey sky. All around the stone was a ring of darker green grass, in a perfect circle. It was really surprising to see the grass so vibrant as late in the year. I was drawn towards it, and couldn't help lean my hand on the standing stone as I tried to keep my balance on the damp grass. I dropped my bag beside it, and leaned over. The stone felt warm to my touch, and I felt a beat of something. Like a low drum somewhere under my feet.

I pulled back from the stone and it was only then that I realised that the weather had changed, so quickly I hadn't time to notice. A low mist curled around my feet, the view that only a few minutes before I'd got lost in, was now lost from sight. The cold settled around me, I was suddenly icy despite my warm clothing, and had lost my bearings. The monument could only have been twenty or thirty metres away and had disappeared completely from view. My breath steamed in the cold air as I stepped backwards on the grass, aware that I was crossing the faery circle and despite the ridiculousness of that, Martha's warning came into my mind.

I tripped over and fell to the ground, my feet feeling like they were being dragged into the soft earth. I twisted slightly and ended up on all fours, the ground again seemed to pull me in. The beat from beneath me grew louder and stronger. I shook my head as if that would stop the noise, and twisted around so I was sitting with my back against the stone. Even though it was damp, the feeling I had was so comforting that I decided to stay there until the mist lifted. The irony was not lost on me, of being in a similar position to what happened at the Druid's temple in Glasgow. The stones, the mist, all I needed was an old man and it would be an identical situation.

At that moment I heard what sounded like a tapping noise, like a cane on rock, followed by the sound of a man clearing his throat.

"Hello my dear, are you there, are you there?" called an old voice. It sounded like the old man from the Temple in Glasgow.

It couldn't be.

"Hello my child, how are you?" He appeared out of the mist, dressed identically, tweed suit, cane and pocket watch tucked into his waistcoat, chain shining. I blinked and shook my head.

This was not possible.

"No, it can't be you!"

"Well that's not a good start for us my girl. How are you?"

It was him, the same man, walking through the mist towards me. He settled down at my side, easily and with the grace and agility of a much younger man.

"What are you feeling about this beautiful temple Kirsty?"

He knew my name. *Why was I surprised? This really felt like magic.*

"How did you get here? This seems a bit mad."

"Just a bit?" He laughed, and the sound was like the wind. There was something so familiar about him. He reminded me of someone, and despite the madness of the situation I suppose my mind was trying to work out if he could have got the ferry over like me, and that this was all real.

I touched the cloth of his coat, and it felt solid. He laughed again, looking at me in amusement. Against the grey stone he glowed in the low sun

"I am real Kirsty, or at least as real as you are. As real as the wind, the rain, the sleet, the snow. As real as the birds, the dolphins, the fish, porpoise and whales. Perhaps it's time for you to ask the question?"

"What question?" Even as I said it I knew what he meant. "What do you want with me?"

"I don't want anything with you Kirsty, but I know someone who does. Will you come with me?"

At that he held out his old wrinkled hand towards me in an age-old unspoken invitation. I knew he'd done it a million times before to a million other souls. The fingers long and bony, without ring or wrist watch. Age spots dripped across the back of his hand covered by what looked like the edge of a blue coloured tattoo. It turned and twisted up his arm, and disappeared beneath his coat sleeve so I couldn't see it properly.

I would have preferred to be anywhere else at that moment in time, and yet I was filled with a mixture of curiosity and obedience. I really didn't want to take his hand, and yet I knew it wasn't really an invitation. It was a command, and one that I couldn't stop myself in obeying. I'm sure I'd survived worse. I had to keep remembering that. I'd been to hell and back.

Touching his hand was like putting my hand into a vortex of bright light, overwhelming sound and a sensation of fast movement. I was aware of extreme heat and something spinning up my arm, strong, tight and bright. Holding me tight like what I imagined a vice to do. I tried to speak but couldn't say a word. The feeling of moving around and around spread to my whole body and engulfed me completely. I had to close my eyes and had a sense of being pulled somewhere, fast. Like metal to a magnet, and I knew I was instantly in another place.

Chapter Seventeen

It was the familiar smell of dampness and decay that hit me first. Even with my eyes closed I knew it was very dark, and also that I was alone. The old man had gone. I had let go of his hand or he had let go of mine somewhere on the journey here. I could hear the sound of water dripping somewhere to my left, it echoed around and there was something else. The wind, I felt a draught playing with my hair and a low boom somewhere beneath my feet. Like a heart beating low and slow. I could feel the vibration like being back at J.J's studio in Scotland. This time though it was quieter and more subtle. There was something else as well, a movement near my feet, and the sensation that I was being watched by a million eyes.

I couldn't avoid it any longer and slowly opened my own, not even realising that I had held my breath whilst waiting to see around me. I was on a pathway of sorts, at the edge of a huge cathedral like space. My toes were over a rocky edge of a huge drop of hundreds of metres. I stepped back instinctively and felt sharp rock biting into my back. Above me and everywhere I could see were what I had thought were huge trees, were dusty and dead looking, traversing down from where they started in a canopy high above my head. It was only as I got closer that I realised that they were tree roots. Faded spots of light squeezed itself through the gaps in the roof and water dripped down like rain to the floor hundreds of metres below me where it ran in rivers and pools of water. I was so high it was like looking down a mountain side through clouds of mist. I knew that the sky was somewhere outside a long way from here. Outside with fresh air, people, light and colour. This place was dark and grey, and everything was in shades of gloom. With a deep breath as I looked around at granite rock and crystal quartz catching the light it came to me. I was inside the hillside, in a chamber within its huge surface. Newgrange would have been hundreds if not thousands of feet above me. Only a few minutes before I had walked around its slope, following the spiralling path, the labyrinth the old man had called it, and now I was inside.

My breath misted around me and I shivered. It was cold, not as bad as outside, but not warm either. The path beneath my feet was hard and I crunched over tiny rocks. On one side was a forest of tree roots, and with it again was that feeling of being watched. I imagined hundreds of people spying on me and that thought pulled me back towards the hillside. Rock and compacted tree roots grabbed at my hair, rough to the touch so I felt it would be safer than walking along the edge. Looking around me I could see that I was on a level area, a walkway. Twisted old tree roots blocked the path and I could not see ahead enough to know which way would be uphill and which way down. Even with that knowledge I didn't know which would be best to take.

If I reached the surface would I be able to get out? I was here for a purpose that much I knew. What it was I still didn't know and that's when I realised. I had asked the old man the wrong question. I'd asked what he wanted with me, instead I should have asked what I was to do. The answer to that might have helped me.

I could walk either right or left, one would surely take me up the inside of the hill, and the other would take me down. Or perhaps both ways led to the same outcome. My head actually hurt with confusion, and I peered into the gloom. A little beam of light dazzled the path to my right and I decided to take that as a sign to move. If I couldn't get far that way I'd just turn around and come back. That seemed the logical thing to do. As I turned my feet on the narrow path I heard the beat beneath me grow louder and faster just for a moment. I wasn't sure if that was good or bad. There was a noise, perhaps only the wind catching against a dried up tree root, and for a second it sounded like high pitched laughter. I shook my head again and started to walk. One foot in front of the other. Watching my balance and trying to avoid the rocks and roots like trees that blocked the pathway. I stayed as far away from the edge as I could, even when water ran down from high above, creating pools on the surface and making it slippy. I kept my eyes on the ground, focused on the task. One muddy foot, lift, put it down, then the other, lift, put it down. My hand on the rock as a guide. Only letting go when I really needed to climb over bigger obstacles, and even then returning to grab onto the rock as soon as I could. My other hand pulling and pushing a way through the thick dusty roots that fell like a curtain blocking the path and the view. My way was slow and ponderous. I knew I was delaying getting to the end. I was heading downhill.

What else could I do?

Behind me I heard a rumble of rock and I pulled into the side, stopping for a moment I took a breath. Even walking downhill was tiring, it was hard to breathe. The dust filled air hurt my chest and burned my throat. I knew I could not stop. It didn't feel safe, with each step, dirt, gravel and small rocks fell over the edge of the pathway, if even that's what it was. I had a sense that not many people had walked that way before. I turned around to try to see what had happened, careful not to twist my ankle or catch my foot in the roots that threatened to trip me up. Tiny grey particles of dust from the dried up tree roots filled the air and I coughed again as it hit the back of my throat, then attacked my eyes painfully. It took a few moments for them to stop watering and then I could see that the pathway behind me had gone. The realisation hit me that I might only have a few minutes before the whole walkway disappeared, and I started to run. Faster and faster, wheezing for breath, too full of panic to stop, in front of me roots and rock tried to slow me though I was determined. I let go of the hillside and used both my hands, my finger nails breaking as I fought wildly through the canopy of roots, forcing my way forward. I heard the sound of thunder inside the hillside as more rock slid down the side. I was in a cloud of dust, and chanced another terrified glance behind me. The pathway upon which I'd travelled had gone, all I could see in the gloom was dust and debris. The landslide was only inches from my heels and running towards me faster than I ever thought I could.

With that thought it reached and overtook me and I was in the air, my arms and legs still pumping like an Olympic athlete, my heart racing at a personal best. Nothing beneath my feet, I dropped like the rocks all around me, my hands grasping out trying to clutch onto anything as I fell over and over, bouncing off soil and roots, through air, mist, water.

My hair pulled painfully, my coat snagged and released, pulled, snagged and released, again and again. I screamed in fear and in pain as my body connected and bumped and bounced hitting against the side of the hill. I called out again and again and even as I did so I knew that no one could hear me as I fell towards darkness and solid rock.

I might have blacked out for a moment, I was still in shock from falling and there was a feeling of being outside my body for a second. I was lying on my side, a huge tree root stopping my progress painfully. My head was on the ground, luckily for me it was soft damp earth. I saw small rocks littering the ground, I'd missed them as I'd landed. Little beams of light flitted across the space, and I was surprised to see bright coloured mosses and grasses, nothing like what I'd seen in the greyness above.

Rubbing my head with bloodied and scratched hands I winced as I struggled to sit upright, my back easing against a large root, so big it was like a huge oak. I wondered how big and old the tree above must have been to send down roots so deep. It was like being in an upside down world. Above my head I could see the canopy of roots and the shards of light that looked like stars in an inky black sky. For a moment I thought I saw the symbol of Archangel Michael and that made me feel better, protected.

Again I had that feeling of being watched. I looked around and was aware of a movement, like the plants and mosses I could see growing around the ground were swaying in a wind. The sound of water tinkling over stones from a little stream alongside made it seem like I was like sitting in a lovely forest glade. Except forests have birds and bees, butterflies and bunnies and other animals. This had none that I could see and apart from the noise of the water, and a rustling of the wind in the roots far above me, there was a very strange silence. I breathed a bit easier down here, there wasn't as much dried dust in the air. And as my eyes grew used to the gloom I could see much more colour, russet reds, greens and blues, and I noticed that everything; the roots, rocks, and plants, everything seemed to move slightly, as if in and out of focus. I rubbed my eyes blinking to moisten them thinking that the dust was affecting my vision. I thought I heard a high pitched laugh again or perhaps it was just the wind blowing off the roots causing them to chime against each other like an invisible natural orchestra of sounds.

I felt a breath on my cheek, someone or something was blowing or breathing hard against me, so close but invisible to see. I felt it on my skin, each cell sensing the tiny changes in air pressure, each hair shifting in the breeze. I heard it, a sound so faint I almost missed it. I peered at the dark tree root closest to me and felt it again. A tiny draught across my face and then a quiet sound like the giggle a small child would make when he was laughing at his own little game. I felt incredibly stupid as I called out.

Is there anybody there? Like I was trying to talk to a ghost in a seance or something a ghost hunter on a crass television show would say. It was stupid, and then the thought hit me.

What if there was a ghost? A terrifying spirit out to do me harm!

I instinctively pulled back so abruptly I hit my head off the jagged root, and snuggled deeper into my coat as if it could protect me. I really was scared, and I didn't know what to do. Tears were close, and I struggled to hold them back, swallowing a couple of times and biting down painfully on the inside of my mouth. I couldn't let panic overtake me. I was here for a reason. I had to wait and see. This whole trip had been about patience, I now had to show some more.

Something touched my head. Rather than scare me, there was a sensation of love, that's the only way to describe it. Someone who loved me had gently stroked my hair, and that reminded me that I was loved and would be looked after no matter how frightening this situation was. I had to keep faith that I'd be ok.

Almost as soon as I said this to myself I was again aware of another breath blowing on my cheek. I stared intently in the direction of the draught and fell back in amazement as I realised I could see a pair of pale amber eyes staring intently at me. Sharp stones bit into my hands and I winced as they took my weight. It's amazing what you can tell when you look deep into a pair of eyes; I saw compassion, I saw love and blinked to break the moment of connection. I realised that I was worried what it would see in mine. For a moment all I could see were those eyes, seeming to float on their own in mid-air, perfectly outlined in their brightness against the dark foliage. A translucent face seemed to materialise around the eyes, I could see a mouth a chin of sorts, followed by a full body shape about six feet in length. It shimmered and moved about in the air around me, shifting its shape formless yet clear and in perfect clarity. The mouth shape opened and I could see its cheeks fill with air as it pursed its mouth to blow at me again. I felt a draught against my cheek. Then the whole body disappeared, one moment it was there, the next nothing, and I was left looking into those amber eyes again. They sparkled and light flashed in them and I knew it would not harm me. I focused on calming down, breathing deep and slow, waiting to see what would happen next. The body appeared again and I could see the whole shape hang in the air I could see through it to the tree roots behind, like an opaqueness rather than a dense material. I sensed that it was the spirit of wind and with that realisation it flowed downwards and disappeared into the water with a splash.

My curiosity edged me closer to the river bank. Holding tight to the edge, the rock and grit biting into my scratched and sore hands I stretched out and leaned over to see a small wave appear in the turquoise blue water. It was so clear I could see the bottom of the river bank where sand and gravel sparkled in the pools of sunshine hitting the floor. The eyes materialised again, or perhaps it was only a trick of the light. The wave rose up and for a moment had a body shape, the eyes in a face of water. It moved so close to me it splashed across my face, like a playful friend would do. The water was cool and refreshing against my skin. It then fell back into the river, splashing over the edge before slipping backwards to join the main body of blue water. Bubbles of white spray fizzed across its surface before it calmed again, becoming so flat I could see in it a reflection of the roof. I sat back on my heels stiffly, rubbing the refreshing drops over my face. I sensed that it was the spirit of water.

I heard or felt something behind me and turned quickly to see that everything was shimmering again. All that I could see had an opaqueness around their edges, like someone had blurred out the sides, those parts where they ceased to be and became something else. I felt something touch my calf and bent down my attention caught by a bright purple plant, its wide fat leaves edged with that same opaqueness. Still wet from the water splashes it took a moment to feel that my eyesight had cleared properly. I blinked again and again. A strange little creature was holding onto the plant and staring at me intently. It was unlike anything I'd ever seen, so small at first I thought it had to be some sort of insect. It had wings I knew that, tiny wings of gold so translucent that I could see through them yet I knew that they were strong and resilient and alive. It had huge eyes in its little face, a long body and thin arms and legs to hold securely onto the plant. Its limbs wrapped tightly around the stem. Its face, it was one of pure intelligence. This was not an insect, and as my eyes really saw it, with a flutter of its wings in what seemed like a gesture to look behind me I was suddenly aware that we were not alone. I slowly turned and gasped in wonder for as far as I could see this whole upside down world was full of these tiny creatures. Most of them were partly hidden, peeking round from plants and rocks and the roots of the trees, in every colour of the rainbow and more. There had to be millions of them all looking at me with the same intelligent expectant expression of the first. Faeries!

I laughed. I threw my head back and laughed. They were magical and as I laughed so did they. Their little laughs echoed around the chamber and they danced and flew all around me, shards of light picking up their incredible vibrant colour like fireflies in the night. It was a dazzling display of fun and laughter and the more I laughed the more they performed. I had to hold my aching sides as it was so funny. The whole space had transformed from somewhere I'd feared into the funniest experience of my life. I had no idea why Martha would have cautioned me against a faerie ring, I would never want to leave such a place, no one would. The little creatures danced and sang and laughed over and over. Their little high pitched voices made me laugh some more. They led each other in a dance around and around the tree roots and before I knew it one of them had grabbed my finger in its hand and I too was dancing along with them, further and further down into the cavern. I had never laughed so much in my life. I didn't know where they were taking me and I didn't care. All my worries disappeared in the laughter. And as my feet danced a path through the bright green moss, and more and more of the faeries joined us I knew I could have stayed there for ever.

Where else would I rather be?

I couldn't stop dancing and laughing. My whole body ached and all I had to do was look around to the faeries and hear them laughing and I was still in their spell. We weaved in and out of the tree roots and with each step along a rock strewn pathway, we travelled deeper into the gloom. They knew their way and I could do nothing else except follow. Faeries sat on my head and shoulders. I felt their tiny fingers and toes holding on to my hair and I couldn't help myself I had to dance, my whole body swayed in a rhythm of laughter. Even as the canopy of roots above me grew denser and the light faded, still we danced and laughed. I was aware of other little flashes of colour around me, deep pinks, violets, intense bright blues, smaller creatures seeming to ride on the wind itself, ducking in and out of each other, watching me intently and happy to be part of our carnival of laughter. They led me into a wider space, the cavern above us huge like a cathedral. Large rocks lay around on the ground, and still we danced, in and out, round and round. I was sore, I was tired and yet still we danced, my feet taking on a magic of their own. I knew

the steps or so it seemed. They flew all around me, pulling funny faces and laughing and I couldn't help myself.
Martha's face came into my mind. She was right. She had
warned me. I had to stop before they took me any further.

I dropped my hand and closed my eyes, covering my
ears with my hands. I shouted loudly to drown out the
sound of laughter. It was all I could think to do. I felt it first,
the atmosphere changed immediately. The faeries jumped
off my head and shoulders. A cold wind whipped across
the chamber, my coat and my hair damp from all the
exertion flew out behind me so strong was its power. The
faeries stopped laughing. The sudden silence all around
me was so abrupt and intense that I knew the faeries must
have been angry and sullen at me. I could feel the change
in the air and very tentatively opened my eyes. They had
turned their backs to me and faced the wall like masters
of passive aggressiveness I thought at first, ignoring me
because I wouldn't play their game any longer. Then I
heard a rumble, a screeching of rock against rock and the
floor shuddered beneath my feet so strongly that I almost
lost my balance, my hands instinctively reaching for something solid to hang on to. The faeries fell to their knees
and touched their heads to the floor, pulling their coloured
wings over their heads in a multi-coloured display that at
any other time I would have appreciated for its beauty. No
one laughed or danced or even moved. They were waiting
for something or someone. I felt the tight grip of darkness
in my gut, a miniscule momentary contraction of my heart
muscle, my breath tight in my chest. I wished I'd kept
dancing. Whatever happened now, this was all my fault.

It was dark, like dusk and I struggled to see into the
gloom. It took me a moment to realise that the wall they

faced towards had started to move. The noise grew louder, bouncing off the rock lining of the chamber, grit, gravel and dried up plants fell on top of the faeries and bounced off their wings and still they sat in silence. I put my hands over my head to protect myself and tried to pull back as quickly as I could. My way was barred by the thousands if not millions of creatures that only a few moments ago had danced and laughed with me so willingly. Now I was completely ignored and what worried me more, I was trapped in a shallow sea of coloured obstacles like fragile shells on a beach. I couldn't have moved without treading on them, and tripping and falling over. Perhaps that's what they had tried to do in leading me here and trap me. I felt foolish. Tricked again.

I turned my attention back to the wall, ignoring the dirt that fell all over me and waited, planting my feet wide on the ground I took a couple of deep breaths to steady myself. I sent up a silent prayer for help. Whatever was coming through that wall was coming for me.

Chapter Eighteen

The silence and stillness of anticipation filled the chamber and I was reminded of my recent dreams. The faeries had not moved an inch. The rock fall had stopped and thick dust still filled the cavern, catching the back of my throat so that I coughed loudly. A warm blast of air hit me in the face, and brought with it a scent of something floral; lavender, roses, flowers in a summer meadow. So familiar and unexpected, and made me feel like home wasn't that far away. I breathed it in, trying to control the feeling of panic. I could imagine my gran close by and I felt calmer. She had once told me not to think that she was dead and gone, instead to imagine that she was in the next room. I found comfort in that idea.

Ahead of me, the faeries started to move. No longer laughing and dancing they quietly pulled back to leave a narrow gap, a multi coloured pathway towards the rock. It was wide enough for me. So I knew that it was an unspoken invitation that I couldn't refuse. I had to walk forward. As I did so I felt the faeries move in behind me, pushing me gently onwards making it impossible for me to walk back. No longer my friends or so it seemed. Heads bent and translucent wings aloft, they were silently obedient. I didn't stop to think who to.

I shuffled forward a few steps, my muscles stiff from the dancing and exertion. My boots crunched across gravel and small stones. I could sense an excitement in the faeries; they must have been pleased that they had delivered me here so easily. My eyes were focused on the rock wall in front of me, and I frantically scanned it for any clue as I reluctantly moved towards it, aware of the creatures moving closer and closer to me. Dust and debris was still in the air, although the rock fall had stopped. I noticed that the faeries had left a space in front of the rock of about a metre. The way they sat in a formation there was a perfect coloured edge, on one side the tiny creatures, on the other grit and dirt, and then the rock wall looming so high above us that I couldn't see the top of it.

A loud boom came from somewhere beneath my feet, and for a moment I was aware again of a beating heart. I felt calmer. I had been told to follow the heart beat and I had in a strange sort of way. Or perhaps it was following me and I knew I was about to find out more.

The ground moved again, less violently this time, and the sound of the heart beat grew louder and louder until it was bouncing off the walls and felt like it was surrounding me. Just like the experience in J.J's studio. A memory of that day reached me and I felt like it was reaching out across time and distance to make me feel better. She had said I was surrounded by love. I had to hold on to that thought, no matter what was about to happen.

The faeries moved back further and further away from the wall, until I stood alone. I didn't dare take my eyes from the wall. I pulled my coat around me in an attempt to soothe myself and to try to keep warm. The temperature had dropped rapidly and I could sense rather than see my breath misting in the gloomy air around me. I shivered, waiting was never one of my strong points. I risked a glance behind me; the cavern was empty. The faeries had all gone, disappeared silently on their beautiful wings. All I could see were the rocks and the tree roots, everything dull and grey in the darkness. I turned back towards the wall, patience was needed again that seemed to have been the theme of my trip to Ireland so far.

I probably stood there for only ten minutes or so, although it seemed much longer. By that time I shuffled from one sore foot to another, and I considered sitting down on the dirty floor to wait, even though it looked hard and unwelcoming. I resisted as I sensed that I was being tested in some way and that I had to stand. The heart beat started to pound again, deep and low, it slowed down and then stopped. The ground shook so violently that the large rocks littering the floor started to move and roll around. I was thrown off my feet onto the hard core landing painfully on my hands and knees. This much be what an earthquake felt like, the whole ground shifting so that you couldn't stand still. I fell backwards and tried to reach out for something solid, and then I realised that nothing was. Everything juddered around, even the largest of the rocks I'd not even taken any notice of before. Now they caught my attention; what if they landed on to me in this bouncing, shaking new world. It was like being on a hard, sharp trampoline, the whole floor hitting me and then flattening out and then hitting me again and again. Even the smallest hard edged stone inflicting terrible pain. It was exhausting and within moments I let go of any kind of control. I screamed over and over again, landing painfully on my front and then on my back the breath forced from me and then bounced again. I was crying I couldn't stand it, I had only wanted to rest on the floor, I thought, not lie down in this earthquake. It was terrifying.

It stopped. Everything was settled and still again, the dust still hung in the air for a few moments longer, then it too rested like me on the floor. Spent, shattered, soaked with sweat and terror still clung to me. I was so incredibly tired but not in a hard worked kind of way, this was the kind of tired that comes after fear and extreme stress. The kind that a good night's sleep doesn't shake off. I was still coughing dust and gasping for breath, it seemed to take ages for my heart to start to beat normally again. My tear stained face red and sweating, every part of me ached. I was warm. No I was hot, really hot, my temperature spiked, sweat ran down my back, pooled at the base of my spine. The chamber had heated up rapidly, I pulled my hands away from the rocks I'd eventually grasped on to. They were now too hot to hold. I heard a loud screeching sound of rock scratching against rock and looked over to where the largest of the stones had come to rest against the wall of the chamber. It had started to move, swinging towards me like a door. And with it the dark of the chamber gradually lightened. Only a few minutes ago behind it had been solid rock. Now I wasn't so sure.

The huge stone came to rest and as I'd expected behind it was a gap in the rock. It certainly hadn't been there earlier. Now there was an entrance way of some sort. I gulped in an attempt to swallow back the lump that had appeared in my throat. I could see a red light, and smoke. I was coughing again, and I started to shake. A tremor of fear ran through me, one I couldn't stop.

I heard loud footsteps as something heavy hit the ground, as it came closer to the gap and then a shadowed figure appeared, silhouetted against the red light. It headed towards me through the smoke. I looked quickly behind me. There was nowhere to go. I stood shivering, my whole body shaking back and forward. The shadow came slowly towards me, long dark cloak billowing, a wooden rod in one hand, and the other hidden in a long sleeve. Its face completely covered in a hood. I knelt on the ground, not knowing if this was what to do, I remembered that's what the faeries had done earlier.

I kept my eyes facing downwards, as it came closer and closer to me. Silent steps, I heard it sniff loudly as if picking up my scent. Like an animal would do. It was only inches away from me now. I could imagine its huge teeth ready to rip me apart as its yellow eyes burned into my soul. This had to be hell. I had been here before, and with that realisation I knew I wouldn't wait for my fate. My patience had gone. I glanced up as the creature threw back its cloak. Adrenalin flooded my system. If I had to fight or run I was ready for whatever I had to do.

Relief flooded through me. The old man stood there, wrinkled hands tightly wrapped around a wooden stick. Smiling his enigmatic smile. As I peered at him in the semi darkness, his face lightened up and seemed to change from a withered old man, to that of an old woman. I blinked and it could have been the way the shadows flicked across his face his deep lines disappeared erased by an invisible hand and he became a younger woman, before that face changed into a young man, becoming younger and younger until he had the face of a young boy, then it became a young girl, a baby, then back again to the familiar old face I'd met twice before. My eyes felt like they were filled with lotion or something that blurred my vision. All around his head was opaque, with his face bright and full of light like he was glowing from the inside. He was the same yet different, more upright, less reliant on the stick. He had more life energy down here, I think that's what it meant. Like he was home. He was still smiling at me, gesturing towards the gap in the rock behind him, which glowed a faint red. My mind was racing.

Could I trust him, then again did I have any choice? My main fear though and the words that kept running around my head almost choking me was what was waiting for me? My heart bumped in my chest, painfully threatening to burst through my ribs. I struggled to stand and realised my legs were trembling too much, like the first time I'd tried to drive without my driving instructor. I'd felt them shake so much I couldn't lift them to the pedals. This was it again. The darkness of fear overwhelmed me and I breathed deep and slow. For a moment I closed my eyes. I needed a second to steady and centre myself.

"Come with me my child. There's someone here who wants to meet you." And with that he held out his hand to help me to my feet and guided me through the hole in the rock.

We entered into a long dark tunnel, high enough and wide enough for us to walk side by side. My boots scuffed across the dirt as I struggled to lift each foot in turn. The sound of my steps bounced off the walls. He still held my arm, guiding me forward, with no sense of urgency, yet we moved quickly and silently. He seemed to glide as if on castors whilst I hobbled along with aching muscles. I felt bashed and bruised like an old piece of fruit. My boots scratched, my coat torn in places.

Within only a few minutes we emerged on the other side into another chamber, much smaller than I'd expected. It looked like it had been cut by hand from solid rock, and was about thirty foot tall and wide. I couldn't tell how deep it was. The back of it was in darkness. No tree roots hung from the roof, nor dirt covered the ground. Instead the walls and floor glittered and glistened as what must have been coal and quartz lit up in turn from the multi coloured lights of thousands of little flying creatures. Like fireflies in a forest I was reminded of again. It was colourful, yet dull, not very bright, and as I looked around and my eyes adjusted to the gloom I noticed that the edges of the space glowed red. Not in a hell kind of way, in a more subtle sun-setting kind of way. It was dramatic, like a stage set for a performance to unfold. I took a deep breath. Setting my feet flat on the floor. My stomach churned. As much as I really wanted to hide behind the old man looking for a safe space, something told me it was time to stand tall. I heard the voice of my old friend Jen

"Fake it til you make it" she always used to say.

I breathed again. I glanced at him and saw that it was as if he was in some kind of trance. Although he stood upright, his eyes were closed. He was as still as a statue. His features looked like they were chiselled from granite, solid and unyielding. He didn't look as though he was even breathing and I would have loved to have nudged him to check. I didn't dare. His cloak had slipped from his shoulders and I could see that he was bare chested. For the first time the tail of a large blue serpent was visible just below the wrist on the back of his hand. It curled round his whole arm, twisting up and completely covering every inch of skin, all the way to his shoulder where its head splayed out. Its long tongue split across the back of his neck, coming to rest on either side of his throat. Even in the poor light I could tell it wasn't a tattoo at all. It looked like it had been painted on to his skin.

I felt the temperature drop suddenly, and could hear a noise from the darkness at the back of the chamber. I couldn't see anything. It sounded like something scratching. The skin on the back of my neck stood up. My stomach churned. I gulped air loudly, my mouth dry, my hands sweating so much I had to wipe them over and over down the sides of my coat. I winced as the cloth rubbed harshly against my already scratched skin and broken nails.

The chamber lightened enough for me to see at the far side of the chamber a large rustic styled wooden door. It didn't fit in with anything I'd seen so far. It made me think that people had visited before me, living and working deep below ground. That someone, perhaps even my dad had been here and left. I had to hold on to that idea. I was getting out of this place. No matter what I had to do, I would get out and see the blue sky and sunshine again. As all these thoughts ran through my mind, the door slowly swung silently open. I blinked and breathed deeply. It stopped, partly ajar, a dull green light shining through.

I glanced towards the old man. He'd gone. Again, he'd taken me so far and then disappeared. In the place where he had stood his cane lay on the floor, with a thick blue rope twisted all around it, the ends lying frayed like a snake's tongue. From the doorway I heard a man call my name.

"Kirsty" He shouted, and for a moment I thought it might be my dad and I almost ran through the partially opened doorway. Until I remembered that Martha had said he'd gone. I stood for a moment, not really sure what to do. Then there was another sound like a drum beating and I could hear a woman crying out, there was something really familiar about that sound. And as if she knew I'd recognised her and she had my attention, she also shouted out my name. Without any other hesitation I pulled open the door and walked through.

Chapter Nineteen

As I stepped over the threshold, the door slammed behind me pushing me forward into a huge space, so big I had to crane my neck to try and see the top. Like the previous chamber, it too looked like it had been cut out from the rock. It was arranged into many levels; terraces joined by pathways and stone steps. It looked like the inside of a huge entertainment arena where you'd go to see a rock band perform. Not what I expected at all. A path led down towards the bottom of the space. I blinked my eyes in amazement as I could see hundreds of little men and women and children. They didn't seem to notice me as they wandered about talking and laughing. Most were about three feet high, and dressed like they had jumped out of a fairy-tale, or I had walked into one. All were dressed in brightly coloured clothing. They wore striped stockings with turned up toe shoes, and little waistcoats and jackets. The women in bright shawls and skirts and hats, hugged their little ones to them. It was a bright busy community.

I wandered down past their tiny round houses built with stones and moss covered roofs. They looked like the dwellings at Knowth I'd seen in the photos back at Angel's house. The ones that lay only a few miles from here on the surface somewhere. Spread out there looked like hundreds of them, and all had little cooking pots sitting on fires in front. Well stacked piles of firewood sat ready beside what I assumed were barrels of water. Filled from the streams that ran down the side of the terraces, into small pools of water. Fenced and gated gardens were filled with flowers, vegetables and fruit trees. Some of the little people were singing and some played hand held instruments that sounded like harps, and drums.

They didn't seem particularly concerned about having me there. I was more interested in them than they were with me, and that helped me calm down. I walked further down the pathway, feeling the vibrations from their drum beats sounding around the place, bouncing off the walls and feeling like it was coming up through the floor. I wondered if that's what I'd been hearing when I was above ground possibly magnified in some way.

There was the subtle scent of flowers in the air, and I could feel a breeze against my skin as I wandered further down-hill through the terraces. It could have been like a summer evening walking in a park, except for the tiny people all around me, and a feeling of unease deep in my tummy. And yet I felt compelled to go on, brushing past the stone houses, my feet crunching over grit and gravel. It was then that I noticed a bright glow from the ground. It seemed to be the only source of light, and as I looked behind me, back along the path and then took in the whole cavern I could see that all the pathways glowed with multi-coloured lights. I stopped for a moment and bent down, my knees cracking so loudly that the little people looked over at me and laughed. I lifted up what I had thought was a piece of gravel, those little rocks I'd been kicking my way through. Holding it and noticing its glisten, sending out a golden light. It was then that I realised that it was actually gold. I had been kicking through little nuggets of gold. As I held another handful of the stones up I noticed different colours and they were diamonds, amethysts, rubies and emeralds.

I stood back up again, careful to drop all the stones back onto the pathway. The sounds all around me started up again as if the people had been watching what I'd do with the treasure. I could feel a collective sigh of relief as I started back along the pathway. There was another breeze against my face, and I was reminded for a moment about the earlier spirit. If that's what it was, I hoped this was a friendly one as well.

Near the bottom of the path, I left the houses behind me and found myself stepping into a flat space, with a rock wall about twenty feet away from me. Its floor was littered with multi coloured precious stones of every colour, and as my feet connected I could feel their energy. And for the first time ever I could hear their sound, as if their vibration had an associated noise. Like a low hum from an engine. It was the sound of aum again. Angel or Grizelle had told me it was the sound of the earth. I got it. I knew what they meant. It wasn't just a sound. It was so much more than that. It was the world.

As I stepped further onto the stones, my feet and legs started to shake so much it was hard to keep my balance. I breathed deeply again and closed my eyes. I had to get over this and I had to trust that it would all work out. It had before, and I had to focus on that.

I opened my eyes and ahead of me a coloured mist skimmed and danced across the top of the stones. It quickly rose up and formed into an archway. A rainbow arch about ten foot tall, and in its centre it glistened like a distorted mirror. I walked towards it, seeing the colours of the crystals bounce off it, swirling, moving around. I got closer, mesmerised by the lights and took a shocked step backwards. Rather than seeing my own reflection in it as I expected, instead I could see the old man. I must have held my breath as I was aware that I let it out in a long deep sigh not quite sure what to do. I was suddenly angry at him. Angry that he'd left me on my own, angry that he like everyone else it seemed, had abandoned me. I wanted to run back to wherever I'd come from and glanced over my shoulder. There was nothing there. All I could see was a mist and a sense that I was alone. The little round houses, the tiny people, everything had disappeared in the mist. The reflection of the old man pulled backwards as well, as if he too was looking behind him. I called out to him, a cry of fear, tears stuck in my throat.

'Please don't leave me, again.' I called out. 'Please'.

I could see him once more, a red light brightening his white hair and whiskers. He nodded towards me and held out his arm again.

I leaned in towards him, my hand hesitating at the edge of the rainbow. For a moment I wanted to know what it would feel like to touch red or blue light. If there would be any difference or even if I'd know that I was passing through a rainbow. The lapse was only momentary, I touched what seemed like a solid flesh and blood hand, warm and strong, and I stepped inside to join him.

I had the strangest of sensations, like being pulled through a psychedelic washing machine at a slow spin. Colours and distorted shapes passed me by. It didn't seem as extreme as before, or perhaps I'd got used to it. Only moments later I was stepping into a huge stone cavern, bigger than all the others put together. I could hear a drum beat. Low, strong, deep, pulsing from beneath my feet and all around me. It bounced off the rock walls and like in JJ's studio, I felt it in my heart and body. I glanced quickly at the old man. He had moved forward and sat down on a rock. It immediately moulded itself to his shape so it looked like he was sitting on a throne. He gestured to me to come closer to him.

I looked around and there was nothing else in the cavern. The walls were as high as mountains. In fact that's what it reminded me of, an old valley I'd once found in the Cairngorm Mountains in Scotland. All around me the mountains had dwarfed me, and yet I'd felt shelter not fear. I had to try and find that feeling again, and ignore the sharpness of the rocks and the feeling of isolation. Even though I stood so close to the old man, I knew he could disappear again at any minute.

He smiled at me, as if he could read my thoughts.

"Are you angry with me Kirsty? Have I let you down?"

I was about to deny it all and then I realised that I had to be honest. What would be the point in lying anyway? He would know.

"Why did you just leave me like that?"

'Sometimes we have to do things on our own. There is no spiritual growth when we sit in our comfort zone, propped up by other people. When the pupil is ready the teacher will come. Think of me as your teacher. You only know your own depth when you face your challenges. Not when you run from them."

My face probably gave away that I didn't agree, before I could say anything he hit his cane on the floor three times. The sound bounced off the walls and if we had been in the

Scottish mountains I wouldn't have been surprised if there had been a rock fall, so loud was it. He bowed his head, his face suddenly solemn and looked like it had been chiselled from stone itself. He slowly moved his hand from his right to left in front of his face, and as he did so, my mind went blank. I didn't have a single thought, instead I heard his voice. He told me that he was sharing his consciousness with me. That I would find it restful and expansive. That he usually has nothing in his mind. This was enlightenment.

I have no idea how long it took his hand to move across. It seemed to me that time stopped and I felt strange. I had no thoughts in my head except the awareness that I had no thoughts, and with that the freedom that I had no worries. In that space I knew that I spent a lot of my time worrying. Worrying about things that had happened, worrying about things that hadn't, and I had a feeling that I wanted more of this empty mindedness.

He might have held me in a spell for a moment or a millennium, I had no idea how long. When I was released I felt refreshed. I looked around the space and found it was filled with creatures, the faeries I'd danced with, the fairy-tale people from the mounds, and others. All smaller than me and in every colour and shape I could imagine and more. The cavern was full of these little people, and they all sat in silence gazing at me. Waiting for me to join them it seemed. Faeries sat on each other's shoulders, in columns of colour. The little people from the mounds sat in family groups. The tiny children sitting on their parents' laps, watching me intently.

I noticed that they had left a space, a pathway in front of me and the old man, it stretched yards and yards in front of us. And all around me I could hear the boom of the earth still beating away.

The old man stood up and held his cane in front of him, and motioned for me to follow him. He walked slowly, head bowed along the path, dust blowing up around his cloak. I kept my head down too, and fell into step behind him. I didn't want him to get too far in front of me. From my side vision I could see the little people's faces as I walked along. Each of them sombre and collected, even the tiniest of the babies, taking in every movement I made. I knew this was important and yet I didn't know why.

The old man stopped abruptly, and took a wide step to his left. I glanced up to see that he had pulled the hood of his cloak low over his head so I couldn't see him at all. He gestured with his cane for me to move forward to stand beside him. As I did so I realised that we'd come to the edge of the cavern, and in front of me was a wide deep ditch in front of the rock wall. I pulled back instinctively calling out loudly, the feeling of his cane on the back of my thighs stopped me. It held me tight wedged between the rocky edge of the floor and the power of his cane. I couldn't move and felt my legs tremor, my breath painfully tight and shallow. In my mind all good thoughts of him gone, instead I was angry at myself for trusting him again.

The cane pushed me forward towards the ditch. My feet slipping and sliding and dust and gravel flew over. I followed their progress as the bounced down the grey sides, so deep I couldn't see to the bottom.

He wouldn't really push me, would he?

By this time I was almost facing the other way, trying to grab onto the cane. I was shouting again at him, sounds of fear rather than words. My heart chilled, I just couldn't keep my balance and my feet kept slipping. I glanced at him again to see that only one hand was holding the cane, yet the power and strength he had was overwhelming and I knew that I couldn't stop him. Even so, I screamed, my arms around the cane. There was no way I was going over quietly.

His hood fell back and I was looking into the face of a stranger. The old man had gone again and left me with a psychopath. I screamed until my throat burned, my feet now jutting out over the edge.

"Stop! Stop!"

And just like that he did. The tension from the cane lessened. I felt it move backwards away from the edge, yet I didn't dare let go, just in case it was a trick and he's push me over when I least expected it.

I threw myself backwards away from the edge. The little people moved out of my way quickly. At that point I didn't care how many I hit, and was contemplating grabbing on to a couple for safety.

The man leaned towards me, throwing off his cape. As he did so I could see he was standing on a rock. He was as small as the others. I wondered if they all had his super strength. That's when I realised how the rock caverns must have been cut by these people. They were indeed extremely strong.

Despite his size there was an aura of authority about him. Beneath the cloak he was dressed elaborately in what looked like golden cloth. His eyes flashed dark green and he stared at me so intently that I had to drop my glance. His features were large in his dark bearded face, with a strong nose and wide mouth. I noticed his teeth were brown and had sharpened points.

He didn't speak to me. As he stared, I could feel his words in my mind. He was the King. He knew my name. Strangely he welcomed me. I didn't know whether to laugh or cry. *What kind of welcome was that,* and as that thought came into my mind I wondered if he would know everything I was thinking. Having nothing in my mind like the old man had done would have been really useful, and as his latest disappearing trick came into my mind I felt my body tighten. I was even angrier at him now. I risked a glance at the King and his eyebrow was raised. He really did know everything I was thinking.

He told me not to be angry. That the old druid was doing his bidding. His fierce stare convinced me that was the case. He welcomed me again. Told me that he had sent for me. And that they needed my help.

It was my turn to raise an eyebrow, and thought to myself, this had to be a mistake, what on earth could they want from me. His answer made me shiver. He said. "You mean, what in earth?"

He moved down from the rock, many men running over to aid him, and I realised that he was possibly very old. In my mind he told me that he was 1800 of my human years old, and that time and age weren't the same inside the earth. He used the cane for support as he walked along the edge, and I knew I had to follow. Questions flooded my mind. He told me that all would be revealed soon, I just had to help him with something first. I felt a weight in the pit of my stomach. He said something about me following my path and I didn't know if he meant that literally or figuratively. I had a really bad feeling as we reached the side wall of the cavern, the deep ditch by our side. The people waiting behind us, the old man gone.

One of his aides shone a piece of crystal towards the wall, and it caught what little light there was to reveal a doorway. A tall wooden doorway like something you'd see in a castle. Edged in metal, dark and solid, it lay partly open. There was something about it that didn't feel quite right, before I could concentrate on what that could be, the King gestured towards it, pushing it further open, and in my mind he told me to enter. I was in the doorway and felt it bang behind me before I knew what was happening. It was then that I realised two things. No one followed me in, and there weren't any handles on the door. I was in complete and absolute blackness.

Chapter Twenty

It took a few moments for my breathing to return to normal. The voice of the King was no longer inside my head. I heard nothing from him. I called out although I knew it was pointless. The huge solid door behind me was designed to keep me in, and I knew that there was no going back. Perhaps I did have to follow a path. That's what I'd been doing ever since starting on this adventure underground. Even above ground I had been walking along pathways. I remembered what the old man had said at the stones in Glasgow. He had talked about walking a labyrinth taking you to another dimension. I'd walked a labyrinth outside Newgrange. Yet the King had told me he'd sent for me so was all of this planned by him in some way?

Why me?

The question bounced around in my head. I took another deep breath. There were no answers coming to mind right now. I had to do something. Even though I knew it was futile I felt around the doorway just to make sure there were no hidden handles or a way to open it. My fingers felt the rough outline of the wood, and metal finishes, nothing else. I paused for a moment, my ear to the door. I couldn't hear a thing from the other side. In the blackness I stood for a moment, listening. For a moment I thought I felt something from behind me. Like a little movement around near my feet. Something scurrying, a sensation against my toe.

I listened again, pulling my coat instinctively around me. Silence. My mind was playing tricks on me. I could have been in a cave, or a huge cavern I had no way of knowing. I spread my arms wide, trying to get a sense for the size of the space. My hands moved through air, nothing solid. I moved away from the door, my arms wind milling around, space. Wherever I was it was fairly large. I moved further away from the doorway, my feet shuffling along, mindful of that deep chasm on the other side. I needed to be careful in case there was a ditch and I'd fall over the edge. I still ached from that earlier helter-skelter of rock and debris. I felt another flutter of something near my feet. I stopped for a moment. Moving my hands upwards. They connected with solid rock. So the place I was in was about 6 or 7 feet or so high. Stretching my arms out at sideways I felt rock. It was about 5 or 6 feet wide. There was nothing in front so I could keep shuffling forward. My feet scraping across the floor, which felt soft like I was moving across mud. I could always come back towards the doorway I counselled myself. I was in some sort of corridor, as long as it didn't get wider I wouldn't get lost. Better to explore than wait for a door that might never open.

It was deep blackness. I couldn't see a thing. I shuffled forward again, and heard a scratching noise close to my ear. There was a strange odour. Strong, more than dampness. Like a sour urine smell. I shrugged. Not sure what it could be. Something ran over my foot. I could feel its tiny feet, each one pushing through the soft suede of my boot, and then the swish as something hit my leg, like a whip.

At the same time something dropped onto my head. I could feel its feet grabbing onto my hair as it tried to balance, its tail flicked across my face. I screamed and ran into the blackness, trying to shake my head and hitting it with my hands like you see people doing with wasps. Except I knew this wasn't an insect. I was cutting my fingers on its sharp rodent teeth. I felt my blood flicking along the pathway. I heard screams as my weight landed on more and more of the creatures. They must have been everywhere. I almost lost my balance so many times as I tried to run faster, my feet connecting with little irate bodies with tails, claws and teeth. I could feel them holding on to my legs, tiny sharp needles bursting through cloth and skin. My breath rasped in my throat, the stinking air filled my bursting lungs. More of them screamed in my ear as they fell on to me as I rushed through the darkness. Tears flowed, mixing with the blood dripping from my wounds. I could feel them land on my shoulders, others pulled at the bottom of my coat, nipping at my fingers drawing more blood.

They were in a frenzy and so was I. My heart pumped in my chest and without thinking about it I was dragging and punching their screaming flailing bodies from my head. My urine soaked hair dragged out at the roots yet I didn't care. Head cleared I pulled my hood up trying to tie it as I ran along, shaking my body as I screamed, feeling them land on me, their little claws dragging into my coat. I ran for ages, bouncing painfully with full force off stone walls, unable to see anything, only the sound of their scratching and the screams in my ears kept me going. I remembered where my fear of rats came from. It was the sound of screaming that reminded me. When I was younger I'd gone with some local boys to a farm where the farmer did his own butchery. The boys took air pistols and set up a shooting gallery at the gutter where the blood ran out of the slaughterhouse and rats gathered to feed. I'd been horrified and ran home to Gran in tears. I don't know what was worst, the rats or the sound of the shots.

I kept running. Ahead of me I saw a chink of light. Instinctively I ran faster. My arms pumping, pulling my cut hands up into my sleeves for safety. It was a doorway just like the one I'd come through and I flew towards it. The light revealing thousands of rats across my path. Eyes glinting, noses twitching, standing up on back legs, teeth and claws sharp and ready to stop me. Some of them as large as cats, I kept going, my feet connecting and kicking and connecting and kicking.

I stretched out towards the doorway, and at the very last moment I saw the ditch lying in front of it. Possibly as wide and deep as the one in the other chamber. The one I'd begged to be saved from. This time I didn't even pause to consider its dimensions. If anything I went faster, my mind seeking any kind of sanctuary and I threw myself across. Everything happened so fast and yet my mind slowed it all down. I had the briefest sensation of the darkness beneath me, a warm draft seeming to push me upwards. My arms and legs pumping mid-air trying to keep my acceleration going. My only objective to leave the rats behind. I landed awkwardly on my right knee, my fingers wet with blood, slipped as I grabbed onto the rock. For an agonising second I felt the weight of my coat pull me backwards and I was out of balance briefly, but my boots found their grip. With relief I dug deep, my arms and legs in agony, I dragged myself fully onto the other side. Out of breath, scratched and bleeding. I was safe. Leaning backwards against the doorway. My whole body twitched as I compulsively relived the last few moments. I could see the rats on the other side of the ditch, screaming, their sharp teeth catching the light, yellow eyes, noses twitching at the smell of my blood. I vomited. My stomach retching at their smell and with the shock. I'd had a phobia about rats for as long as I could remember. That had been my worst nightmare.

I knew I had to move onwards, now there really was no going back, and behind me the doorway lay partially open in invitation. I glanced across the ditch and saw that the rats had started to climb down the side. I could hear them scratching their way down the rock. No matter how deep it was, it wouldn't be long before they found a way across. I used what felt like the last of my strength to crawl through the doorway and banged it shut behind me. It was solid wood and had a metal bar I could use to latch it. As I pushed it into place I could hear the sound of scratching on the other side. They'd already found a way over.

I wouldn't be safe for long. I knew it, I took a moment to take a breath. My hands nipped. I could still smell them and feel the sensation of them in my hair. That had been horrific. I hated rats. Being eaten alive by them was one of my biggest fears, such a gruesome way to go. I heard their sharp little claws working their way through the wood of the door. As solid and thick as it was, they'd get in. I knew I had to move.

I could hear their outraged screams, and it seemed like their scratching was getting louder. It was awful. I shook my head again in a vain attempt to clear the sound.

It was then that I realised that the sound of scratching came from behind me.

Chapter Twenty-One

my first thought was the rats had outsmarted me and found a way in to the chamber. I'd been so relieved in that moment, believing that I'd survived my worst fear, that it hadn't dawned on me that there was any other way for them to get in. I hadn't for a moment considered that they had outsmarted me. The rats had won. I was about to be devoured and no one would ever know what had happened. I whimpered, a physical pain seemed to stop me from breathing properly. I turned my head and as I did so I realised that I could see in the dim light that came from somewhere to my right hand side. This chamber was lighter. I was no longer in darkness and I knew that I'd see them eating my fingers, my toes and I would see and feel every bite until I died. I had no breath or energy to scream.

My eyes took in all of the space I could see. The edges faded into darkness. The rats hiding there, taking in my every tense, terrified movement. I slowly turned around, wincing at the movement, my muscles and skin screamed in my mind. It was impossible to know the size of the chamber. Scratching came from all around me, bouncing off the walls I assumed were also hewn from the rock. The earthen floor on which I sat was full of ruts and scratches.

I'd inadvertently ran into the rats' den. The shadows hid my tormentors, taking their time it was as if they were playing with me, smelling my fear.

And yet my mind was still working out a way. The light had to lead somewhere. *What choice did I have?* Give into the rats I'd already evaded, and wait for them to finish with me. *Or did I dare to run again?*

My muscles tensed again, every bit of energy I could find sent rapidly to my limbs, I was ready to flee as fast as I could. It was then I heard a growl. A low, spine shattering growl joined by another and then another. From the shadows, lit for only a moment, so fast I thought I'd imagined it, I saw a long clawed paw. Yellowed claws, sharpened on the very earthen covered floor I crouched upon, ready to run. The realisation hit me that I wasn't surrounded by rats in this chamber. It was something much worse. I heard another growl, closer to me this time.

My hand sat partly in the shadow, leaning down heavily into the damp earth. I paused to look at it for a moment, and as I looked up I caught a flash of yellowed teeth, a snarl, a growl on the biggest wildest dog like creature I'd ever seen. It was all I needed. I didn't wait another moment and threw myself forward towards the light. I scrabbled for a moment running on all fours as I fought to stand erect, then ran as fast as I could. Again, my arms and legs pounded along the ground. I didn't dare look behind me from the yelps, barks and growls I knew there was a pack at my heels. They might have been faster than me over open ground, my mind told me that there was a chance. This was still a confined space of some kind so they couldn't get past. At least I held on to the faint thread of hope that was true. It's all I had. I don't think I even took a breath. I did nothing that had the potential to slow me down. Head down, coat flying behind me I ran faster than I'd ever done before.

I followed the light, careering around corners, bumping into walls as I ran. Scratched, bleeding more, my knuckles grazed on rock. Ahead of me I saw the chamber had opened up wider. I sensed dogs running to my left and right, and saw the shadows of their bodies, tails and ears on the rock walls on either side. Huge monsters, they planned to overtake me. Take me down as prey. How long had they waited for food? I could feel them nip at my coat, each contact designed to slow me down so powerful were their jaws.

I kicked something and in the half light realised I was running across a field of bones. There was no time to react to the horror of it all. I remembered I'd been chased by a pack of wild dogs before. On holiday in India in my twenties, walking along a dirt track with a friend. Too nervous to call a taxi we'd decided to walk, and within a few moments been surrounded by a pack. They'd smelled our fear as we'd tried to walk along, picking up the pace. The dogs came closer and closer to the back of my legs. I felt one continually nip at my shorts and remembered the cold fear I'd felt in case they bit me. This was the same. We'd been saved by an Irish man and his sister who'd appeared like angels and hissed them away. Kicking the one closest to me so that it yelped and the others had followed it back to the shadows of the night. Funny that he had been Irish. He'd said you had to use a pack mentality and go for the leader, do something unexpected. I'd forgotten all about that until I was in the same situation. How much I yearned for an angel to help me.

I could feel my energy waning, the last of my adrenalin had drained away. My vision blurred, I had a pain in my side. To my right I saw a pale blue light. Without thinking about it I stopped sharply and started towards it, I was running on empty. I knew I couldn't go much further, yet something compelled me to force my body with the very last of my energy towards it.

So abruptly had I stopped and changed direction that the dogs were confused for a moment and I could hear them yelp as they bumped into each other. Their claws scratching deep into the ground as they tried to balance as they followed my sharp turn. From the side of my eye I saw their yellowed teeth, drool dripped mouths, blood lust. It was all the time I needed to throw myself towards the glimmering turquoise light. My panicked brain was able to note that it came from a hole cut from the rock, and it was big enough for me to push myself inside. As I banged painful shoulders against the opening I was incredulous to see a metal gate, folded back against the wall. I slammed it shut behind me. It had a key which I quickly turned with hands that shook so much I could hardly control them, just as the dogs snouts and teeth snapped through inches from my hands and face. Howling in outrage they banged against the rusting structure trying to force a way in through the metal struts to where I lay back on the ground, panting. Exhausted. Emotional. I had nothing left. I had to trust that the old gate would hold them back, because I knew I wouldn't be able to run again if they did break it down.

Unable to reach me, they whined, barked and continued to throw themselves against it. And I could see them, at least a dozen, possibly more. All large and powerful, wild eyed and uncontrollable. I loved dogs but these weren't your usual family pet. These were crazy, starved and determined.

Despite the gate's fragile appearance, it held securely, the key rattled around in its lock every time they hit it forcefully. There was no way I could have leaned against it, as their paws and jaws stretched to reach me. I was relieved when after a few terrifying moments where I winced with every shudder, they fell back into the shadows beyond the light. I heard them fighting, barking, growling and snapping at each other before the sounds started to fade away. Trying to catch my breath, I was scared for a moment to look around me, given the last two experiences. I waited until I could hear nothing from the dogs before I chanced a glance over my shoulder, although even that small movement was agony. I'd done two hard sprints within a few minutes of each other, my whole body was tightening up, and I had started to shiver. The hair at the back of my neck, was cold and damp.

This was a smaller chamber than any I'd entered so far and I was relieved to see that it was bright and most importantly was empty, or so it seemed from my quick glance. There was a strange echo like you get at an indoor swimming pool, and I could hear water dripping. Rather than darkness the whole place was filled with a pale blue light. It dappled across the roof and all around the walls, catching some flint or quartz so that the whole place glowed. As I turned round I saw that the light was coming from a large lake of water in the middle of the chamber. Lit from below, the water shifted in colour from blue to green and turquoise, and then played out that palette all around the space.

I dragged myself closer to the water and found the rock floor was covered in a layer of golden sand, so I laid back on it, my coat hanging off me. My damp hair splayed across my face. Every part of my body ached, and my scratches from the last few hours nipped. I wanted to sleep, just close my eyes and give up. I was exhausted, in a place almost beyond it. It was like I didn't really care anymore. I had no idea where I was or how I could get home. I breathed deeper and noticed that it was the sort of smell you get at the seaside. Fishy and salt water mixed with seaweed. I took another deep breath. It was like being at the beach. A strange underground beach of course, and I soon had that restful feeling I get when near water. Although the last time I'd been at the sea, I'd had the baby whale in my arms, and that not even twenty four hours before.

The air was full of calm and peace, and just by breathing I felt I was filling up with positive ions. The tranquil colours and the light were restful. I leaned back, stretching out, feeling some warmth coming from the sand beneath me. I had a sense that I needed to recharge my energies as best I could. Strangely I wanted to sleep, and I was in that space between awake and asleep when I heard a splash from the water behind me. For a moment I wondered if I wasn't alone after all.

Chapter Twenty-Two

I stiffly turned over to my stomach, still stretched across the sand which had become deeper and warmer beneath me. I was close to the edge of the pool of water and noticed how clear it was. On the far side were large rocks, and some waterfalls of the brightest blue meandered downwards. Rainbows appeared in the slight mist that rose from the water. I couldn't see anything else in the chamber, and there didn't look like there were any shadows to hide anything sinister. I leaned over and pushed my hands into the water. It was warm like a bath, and I watched the blood and muck wash away. I sensitively patted my face and head to try and cleanse my wounds. Strangely it soothed me, and as I pulled my hands from the water I noticed that my cuts and bruises had faded away, and I could no longer feel any pain. A deep sigh of pure astonishment and relief escaped me, and feeling better and braver, I took a deep breath and pushed my whole head under the water.

I ran my hands through my hair, the water soft like silk. I washed away the dried blood on my head and as my fingers rubbed and my scalp I felt that all my cuts had healed. Pain free and clean, I wondered if I could dip my whole body in and how good that would feel.

I pulled out of the water, squeezing and shaking out my curls, instantly refreshed and revitalised. I heard a splash on the water again and glanced quickly up at the rocks. I blinked the water from my eyes, my vision blurred for a moment. There was a flash of green, at first I thought a trick of the light, and then a louder splash, and the feeling of warm water hit my face. A playful gesture like the one from the riverbank before I met the faeries. That seemed like a very long time ago.

I peered into the water, and felt a splash again. I still couldn't see anything. I sat up on the sand, pulling my dripping hair back off my face. A rainbow moved down from the rock, playing across the surface of the water, where a slight mist had appeared. I found myself breathing deeper as I watched the rainbow stretch out and cover the pool, so it had a covering of light translucent colour. I leaned in and pushed my hand into the water, feeling a vibration as I cut through red and yellow air, orange and indigo and violet. As I tried to push through the green and the blue it felt different, thicker. Like moving from milk to marshmallow, and I felt the colours move away from my fingers. It was strange, and pulled my hand from the water. Sitting back on my heels I wasn't sure what to do. Another splash hit me on the nose drawing my attention back to the pool.

The mist had parted slightly and the green and blue colours from the rainbow twisted round into a circle, darted across the water, transforming into an arc, and then back to a circle again, before splashing deeply into the centre of the pool. As I stared the mist parted again and I was looking at a woman. At least the top half of a beautiful woman, she had palest green hair, almost the colour of the water as it changed in the light. It fell across her upper body in long curls, from a dazzling crown made from shells and golden seaweed. Garlands of shells surrounded her neck and arms, her eyes were large and the deepest green. She was smiling at me as if she recognised me, holding out her arms towards me in welcome.

I fell back in amazement. I started to ask her who she was and how she'd got there but she turned her back on me, and sunk beneath the surface, her hair floating across the water for a moment before she disappeared from view. It had to be a trick of the light along with dehydration and all my exertions I thought, and then she reappeared again. Rising higher and higher out of the water like she was on a platform powered by Neptune. Water dripped from her skin, her hair bounced up in waves and curls, covering her nakedness. She held her arms out towards me, and smiled deeply. In her left hand was a pink conch shell, the kind that people hold to their ear to hear the sea. She held it out for me to take, tantalisingly out of reach.

I called to her, and she once again turned her back to me and sunk into the water. This time she disappeared for a couple of minutes and I called out to her, concerned that she'd drown. When she didn't come back up I stepped into the shallows at the sandy edge, oblivious to my boots, clothes and coat, as I peered into the clear water trying to find her. Standing in the water was usually a worry for me. I had a fear of deep water so I always swam in swimming pools. I rarely ventured into the sea on holiday. My concern for her was such that I didn't really care.

Her beautiful head cleared the water again with a splash, further away from me, closer to the centre of the pool. She said nothing, still holding the conch out to me, as a gift I thought. Water dripped from her and reflected from the tiny shells and golden seaweed draped across her hair and body. She was so very beautiful, mesmerising, exotic, holding her hands out in welcome, bearing a wonderful present.

My eyes settled on the conch. I so wanted to hold it to my ear to find out if I could hear the sea. Yet another thing I'd heard of, and never tried. It glowed, light reflecting from its shining surface. I held out my hand towards it, and she moved closer to me, her other hand reaching for mine.

Rising steadily higher and higher in the water, for the first time I could see her fully, and noticed the turquoise coloured scales covering her from the waist down to her tail. The hair, eyes, smile, and her sculpted arms and hands covered in jewellery from seaweed and shells. She was so very beautiful, and I knew from her gift and her smile that she was kind and caring. She wanted to take care of me. I was oblivious that as I stretched towards her outstretched hand I was already waist high in the water.

I don't know if I moved to her or she moved to me, I felt a slip as my feet missed a step. I felt her icy cold hand, and as I reached out to grasp the conch, my coat was already filling with water. I was dragged under the surface, and instinctively kicked out backwards, dropping the conch. As I coughed and spluttered, spitting out water and tried to catch a breath, I saw it fall beneath me.

I looked at her quickly, she was still smiling at me, the light reflecting in her beautiful eyes. She held her other hand towards me, and I took it gratefully thinking that she would support me in the water, and let me collect my breath. It too was cold. An icy cold that was such a surprise I called out to her. She smiled at me in welcome, so very beautiful. Her grasp was tight like a vice and I tried to ask her to relax it a bit as it was so strong. Both my hands were now in hers, and she very gently and gracefully slipped beneath the surface again. This time holding on to me so that I couldn't get away.

I was still spluttering and had only a moment to grab a very quick breath. I expected her to pop back up to the surface again so I didn't really take my situation seriously. She had been so very welcoming. Under the surface of the water I saw her clearly as she smiled at me, her eyes still bright and wide, her hair billowing all around her, so beautiful. The grip of her cold hands in mine tightened, and she slowly and sleekly dropped further beneath the surface, taking me with her.

I needed to breathe. The air in my lungs had more determination to force out than I had to keep it in. My whole face contorted. I pushed my tongue at the back of my teeth to try to hold my sacred breath inside. The power of the breath, that instinctive force that keeps us alive was impossible to battle. Bubbles of air escaped my nose, I could see them my precious life force escaping from me in the beautiful icy blue water. I tried to signal to her that I was in trouble, rather than help all she did was smile wider as she held my hands tightly, slowly, certainly and powerfully, she dragged me deeper. I tried to pull my hands away from her but her strength was incredible. I tried to kick away from her and that too was impossible. I didn't dare cry or make any noise as I was terrified to lose any air. And yet the light below us was brighter than the light above. I started to feel confused.

Had I missed her turning and twisting me upside down and we were moving back towards the surface. Was I was panicking over nothing? Relief rushed through me. I could hold my breath for another moment. I'd be safe soon. It had been a prank, just a trick. She had been so lovely. She still was. My vision was clouding, blood vessels bursting in my eyes as I looked across the short distance between us.

My body started to automatically convulse, pain in my stomach, lungs, head and throat. I felt my back arch, no longer aware of the weight of my coat or the chill from her fingers as she dragged me down. I realised that this was real. There was no joke. There was no escape.

The last of my breath was forcing its way out I cried, no longer any point in holding it in, my head jerked backwards and yet still she smiled gracefully, her eyes full of joy as they sparkled in the light. After everything I'd done, everything I'd come through and this was my end. My body shook violently, there was a darkness around the edge of my vision, it blurred with the last of my tears. A shooting pain stabbed me in my head, and my lungs screamed for mercy. All I could see was her smile fading into the shades of deepest blue.

It was so cruel, my body unable to do a thing except buck and buckle, and yet my mind was able to take it all in. As I witnessed what was likely to be the last of my air bubble its way to the surface, I gave up. I stopped fighting. I wanted to scream at this smiling assassin, the one I'd trusted, that I was done. I had nothing left to fight with. I'd out ran everything they'd tested me with and now I knew I couldn't do it anymore. My arms sagged, I threw my head back and felt the rush of water as it forced itself into my nostrils. I opened my mouth, I wanted her to hear me shout. And as I did so I realised something, as I was held there in the water, somewhere between the bottom and the surface, between living and death. I realised that I'd run from it all, like I'd always done. I'd rarely faced anything in my life. A tiny moment of reflection and self awareness. I was so incredibly sad at the life I'd wasted. All the time I'd given my power to someone else, to situations that didn't serve me, and that didn't make me happy. I'd spent so much of my adult life going through the motions of what I thought life should have been rather than creating my own. My gran had tried to tell me so many times not to care what people thought. For the first time I really got it. None of it mattered. She used to say a funny thing. She'd say that what people thought of me wasn't my business, and I thought she was mad.

Another thought came into my mind of all the times I'd tried to control things. Truly believing that I could control anything now seemed ludicrous. I wanted to laugh and cry, all that effort to get me here, and I'd blown it. She used to say that I'd be guided if I just took a moment to trust, and again I thought she was wrong. Except it had worked for her. She'd been so trusting in life, the earth and the heavens. I'd always resisted anything that wasn't practical and fitted in with my idea of control. Yet that hadn't worked for me either. Perhaps it was time for something else rather than resistance. It was time to surrender. There was nothing I could do anymore. The water rushed into my lungs, and my whole body was taken over in spasms. I saw the light rising up to meet me, and panic softened into peace in my heart, I felt strangely connected and surrounded by light. And as I closed my eyes I knew that there was something relaxing about not having to try anymore.

Chapter Twenty-Three

Another spasm ripped through my body, my lungs now filled with water. I looked around me, we were deep below the surface. She still held my hands, with less pressure than from before. We continued to move downwards. I was breathing, or at least the water came in and out of my nose and mouth, and I was still conscious. She smiled at me again and for the first time I was able to smile back. She laughed, and I heard the sound of it like water dropping over stones. Her cool hands squeezed mine, and I returned the gesture. There had been no need to panic and cry. I should have trusted her. I should have trusted my first instincts. Whatever was going on in this crazy upside down world, the laws of the land and sea as I knew them were not valid in this place. We continued to spiral downwards in the crystal clear water, eyes locked.

My feet hit the bottom of the water, and she moved me towards the side where my shaky legs walked across dry sand. Looking around me in wonder I was back in what looked like the same cave. The blues from the water flashed across its wall and roof. It was the strangest thing. I'd definitely gone into the water. I had no way to know what had happened. Like breathing under water, none of it should have made sense and yet it did. She splashed behind me and sat on a large rock. I coughed water from my lungs, rubbing my hands over my wet hair and clothes. Within only a few moments I was completely dry.

I was facing the gate, which now lay open. I walked towards it, hesitant and listening for a growl or any other sound. There was silence, so with only a quick glance back towards the mermaid, she nodded and I stepped into the corridor. Ahead of me was a large wooden door, studded with metal, again it lay partly open. I pulled it wide and stepped through into a huge chamber. The biggest I'd been in so far. It was like a cathedral, greys and silver walls cut from rock. At first I thought huge trees held up the roof and as I looked closer I could tell they were intricately carved, colossal pillars of stone. I guessed that the whole place had been chipped away by hand. From where I stood I could see the marks tiny hammers had made, and I thought about the little people I'd seen and wondered if they'd done it.

The edges shimmered with a faded green light, and as I squinted I could tell there were hundreds and thousands of little lamps all around the space. It stretched way into the distance. There wasn't enough light for me to see clearly to the other side. I could hear a deep beat. Like the sounds I'd heard so many times in the last few days. I had a sense that I would soon find out where it was coming from. It bounced off the high walls so that it was all around me. Almost like being in a womb hearing the mother's heartbeat. With that thought, I took a deep breath, flattening my hair, fastening my coat. I was shabby and scratched yet I had survived it all. I now needed to know more, and I suddenly had an overwhelming urge to find out why it had happened to me.

I moved further into the chamber, my steps on the stone floor bounced off the high walls and echoed so it seemed like there were hundreds of people around me.

Or with me. I realised.

What this whole experience had taught me was that I was resilient, a survivor, and I was protected by someone or something, so why would I worry about every little thing that happened to me. Did I feel connected? Yes I did. Did I feel protected? Yes I did. With each footstep my inner voice whispered powerful words of encouragement rather than my old habit of negative self talk. It was like having a very best friend with me, a cheerleader who told me how well I'd done and how far I'd come. For the first time I believed it. I felt stronger. I had no intention of running away again. My brushes with death made me realise that when it was really my time to go, it would happen and there was nothing I could do about that. I wish I'd known that years ago.

A mist swirled up around me, and without any hesitation I walked faster, purposefully into it. I needed answers. My footsteps sounded loud and determined. Whatever was waiting for me would know I was coming.

The mist cleared as quickly as it had arrived, and in front of me stood the King. All around him the little people, and the faeries sat in multi coloured rows, thousands of them all watching me intently, in silence. Their big eyes full of wonder as if they were looking at something magical. I looked around for the old man and couldn't see him. The creatures had pulled back to leave an aisle for me to walk along towards the King. As I passed each, they bowed low, eyes to the ground. He smiled at me, and welcomed me back. He held out his gloved hand and I knew I had to bow and kiss it. Brushing my lips across what smelled like leaves from an old tree.

Close up he looked so much older than I'd thought he looked before. He moved aside and motioned behind him, and told me that it was time for me.

"Time for what?" I asked out loud and I heard all the creatures sigh. Perhaps I wasn't supposed to ask any questions, now I needed to know more and I didn't want to wait much longer.

He gestured me to move over towards the centre of the chamber, and as I walked along the faeries moved back from me, in a multi coloured display of military precision. Each of them fluttering backwards to take the place of the one behind them. It was like watching a butterfly fluttering its wings. I kept walking. The beating sound got louder and louder, bouncing around the space. The green light bathing us all in an ephemeral almost underwater glow. Strangely the water had indeed taken away all my aches and pains and I felt energised. I knew that the King would tell me when to stop, or I'd find where I needed to be. I realised again that I didn't have to worry.

Towards the centre I could see a large stone mound. It looked like a miniature version of Ayers Rock, Uluru in Australia. Just like the rock it glowed red and was flattened across the top. As I got closer I could see some steps had been cut in its side, so without hesitation or waiting for permission I set my foot on the first one. Immediately I felt as if the air had thickened. It was like walking through water, and as I climbed the twenty or so steps to the top, my feet grew heavier. By the time I reached the top I had to drag my legs along as if I was in mud up to my waist.

I stopped, and was struggling to breathe. I felt heavy. I was considerably higher than the others, and as I tried to look over the edge to see them they disappeared in a swirling green mist. I waited, and that's when I realised that the beating sound was coming from under the ground at the very place where I stood. I remembered what Grizelle had said to me what seemed a very long time ago. She'd told me to follow the sound of the beating heart. However I'd done it, I was exactly where I needed to be. The rock shook beneath me, as if in acknowledgement.

I heard a woman call my name, loudly, each syllable bounced off the walls. For a mad moment I thought it was Grizelle, but she was miles away. The voice was deep and commanding, someone used to giving orders and it reverberated around the chamber.

"Kirsty, welcome home."

I didn't know what to do or say. I looked around me trying to pinpoint where the sound was coming from, expecting to see a large lady stepping up onto the rock. No one appeared.

The voice called out again.

"Kirsty we want to welcome you. We are so happy that you are here with us. It is time."

"Time for what?" I asked, and then the question that had burned in my brain for ages. "Why me?"

"It had to be you."

"Who am I talking to?" I asked. "Tell me that first."

"Don't you know Kirsty?" There was almost amusement in the voice. "I am."

That's all she said. "I am". And she said it in such a definite way that I couldn't ask another thing. I had a sense that she was everything. Earth, water, air, spirit. Everything. I tried to kneel down in case my legs started to shake. My heart rate had spiked I could feel it bouncing in my chest and I was hot. Breathing was hard as if all the air had sucked away all the oxygen. As much as I wasn't scared in my usual way, I'd had enough of fear to last me a lifetime, I felt strange. That's when I realised that I had no feeling in my legs. I couldn't move them at all. The heaviness I'd felt as I walked up the stairs had transformed into a solidness I'd never experienced before. Like my legs were encased in concrete.

I looked down to see that the rock had risen up to meet me, and now fitted around my waist. I hadn't felt a thing as it slowly and gently entombed my bottom half. I pushed against it, trying to squirm my way out but it was impossible. I was set in the stone as surely as if I'd dug a hole and filled it in. I took a deep breath.

Was this what the King had meant when he said it was time?

I took another deep breath. I tried to ask inside of myself like I'd been told to do. They wouldn't bring me through all of this without at least telling me why. It wasn't my time to die. I focused on that. A slight waft of a floral fragrance reached me, and I breathed deeply. I was calmer.

"You are here because we need you." The voice continued, no mention of my predicament. "We have waited a long time for you to be born."

The voice bounced off the walls, along with the boom from what had been beneath my feet. Now it felt like it was all around me. I stopped squirming, realising that I'd be free when it was time.

"It is time."

Despite my best intentions, my heart rate spiked in shock and my breath became shallower. I looked around the space, suddenly realising that the mist had risen higher. I could no longer see the rock walls or ceiling. The only sense available to me was sound, and that made her voice all the more powerful.

"It's taken a long, long time for you to be ready. We have waited patiently. We need you to communicate for us."

A wind blew sharply, with such force that my hair stood on end, it parted the mist in front of me. At the same time the rock glowed fiery red, like embers had been stoked, and I could see to the far side of the chamber. In a circle stood eight colossal thrones, carved from the rock. The space was huge. I could distinguish the intricate carvings that snaked up the walls and covered the thrones in symbols that I recognised. Similar to those I'd traced with my finger on the standing stones outside Newgrange. On each throne either leaned or sat a giant man. All eight were dressed in what looked like ancient styles of clothing, some wore crowns, others wore helmets, one had horns on his helmet like a Viking, a couple had long flowing hair and beards. Their craggy faces looked exhausted, dirty, encased in mud and what could without have been dried in blood.

Each of them raged, and thumped the armrests of their thrones, one or two jumped up for a moment, on foot they were bigger and more brutish. Their fingers stabbed and jabbed at an invisible enemy. These men were angry. I could feel their temper from where I stood, hundreds of metres away from them, and flinched as I watched the raw emotion flicker across each scarred face. They were huge, contorted and locked in a battle in their minds. Each of them sitting so close, and completely oblivious to each other. One carried a spear, other's had gigantic swords in their hands or resting close to them. The metal hand of one of them caught the light and it dazzled my eye.

"These are the ancient kings of Ireland. They have been called the Giants of Old. They are stuck in the anger of their times. In a space of eternal struggle and suffering. They are unable to let go of their violent pasts. Trapped in their old lives, re-enacting every battle, every betrayal, continually. It has been like this over and over for thousands of years so far. That anger is trapped in this land as well Kirsty. Human kind cannot evolve whilst this energy remains. You are all connected. Change this and we change everything."

"What do you see behind them Kirsty?"

My eyes were so focused on the kings that I had not looked anywhere else in the chamber. When she said this to me I dragged my view from the one sided battle scenes in front of me, and looked around. As I watched, I realised that I could see a glistening behind them, like a shimmer of gold. As I looked closely I started to distinguish within it, figures appeared and then faded away. The more I focused the more the faint apparitions of men, women and children appeared. What struck me was that they all wore the same expression of sadness. I could feel their grief and as I watched I saw them holding their arms out towards the kings, as if beseeching them to turn around, before they turned away and then back to try again.

My grief was so recent and raw that I felt the emotion of it, and wiped tears from my eyes. My heart full of pain for these ignored souls who seemed to care so much for the kings. I realised that they were all trapped. The kings never venturing from their thrones, the shimmering souls trapped behind an invisible barrier unable to reach them.

"Why can't they come closer?"

"They are souls, full of love. They cannot cross the barrier of anger that surrounds the kings."

"But if the kings turned around, surely they would see them?"

"The kings are stuck looking at that aspect of their past that they most associate with. The souls are their loved ones, and their descendants, all who came after them are trapped too. They cannot see them, they cannot hear them, and they have no awareness of them. It is here as it was when they all lived. The kings' focus was on warfare and violence, not on love nor kin. They are stuck in their past lives, and so are their descendants."

I felt such an overwhelming sadness for them all as I looked at the shimmering souls begging for attention, and the kings trapped in their circle of anger and hate. It was no wonder that it was stuck in the land and with us.

"Is there nothing that can be done?"

Even as I asked I had a sudden premonition, a knowing that this was why I was here. Rather than scare me, I wanted to try.

"We had to test you Kirsty. The rats, the dogs, the Murduchann mermaid. We have waited a long time for you to be born, but we needed you to know that you could do this. Hence the trials you have had to endure, to prove it to yourself. It's always been the way. You endure hardship so you can build resilience. Humans get stuck in the past so often. Now it is time for change. We cannot wait any longer. For us all, for both the physical planet and the energetic earth we all call home it is time to change. We have to do it now. For the safety of everyone and everything. Now you are ready."

"Why now?"

"Descendants of the kings have created new technologies that are affecting all of us. A new vibration that matches our earth song. The beating of my heart. It is so powerful that it could move our solar gate out of alignment, not just here but all around the world. The Other World, under the earth dwellers need the light that comes in at the solstice to survive. Everything is balanced, if they do not survive neither do those who live on the surface. This cannot continue."

"What's the solar gate? Is that what you call Newgrange?"

"Newgrange is one of them and one of the most important. We need the stones there to be safe and stable. Otherwise the gate can't awaken."

The lovely face of Guy from Glasgow flashed into my mind. He'd been working on the sonar technology, was that what she meant? He had said he was descended from Irish kings. I hoped that he'd be ok, whatever happened.

I'd felt such a connection with him on the boat. I knew he'd want me to do the right thing. The air was still and quiet, a faded scent of flowers reached my nose, my body felt strong.

"What do I have to do?"

"Not do. It's what you have to say. Unlike you, the kings cannot hear me. I need a human to speak to them for me. You and I are connected. We always have been. It is has to be this way. It is time to release the kings and the earth from the violence of the past."

As she said that I felt the beat beneath me deep and slow, and I realised that it was in time with the rhythm of my heart. My hands moved down to rub my stiff legs so I'd be ready to run. And that's when I remembered that I was completely encased in rock all the way to my waist.

"We are one Kirsty. You have my strength. I have your voice."

I coughed. It was a tickle at the back of my throat. I coughed again, harder this time trying to clear it. The rock started to rise, and with it so did I. Higher and higher it pushed me up, and at the same time we moved closer to the ancient kings. The whole rock had shifted, silently and smoothly so that within only a few moments I was eye level with them.

I cleared my throat roughly, and the voice and words that came out were not from me. I could hear the earth speak through me.

"Ancient Kings, hear me now," I cried deep and loud. "Hear me now."

"I call upon your ancestors, I call upon your descendants, Great Kings, hear me now."

With this there was a rumble and the whole cathedral like chamber quaked, rocks and gravel slid down the sides into huge piles of debris, hundreds of feet below me. They stopped and stared at me. I could see shock and disbelief flash across each of those big, scarred faces. Distracted from their warmongering they saw me. A tiny human woman at the top of a huge rock, with a voice that filled the chamber.

Behind them the souls turned towards me and fell to the ground, their hands grasped in prayer looking desperate. I could hear their cries for help.

"Hear me, the earth is speaking. Those stone thrones are but shackles that hold you to this ground, where you no longer have a place. This is all but an illusion, a fallacy born from your determination to control and dominate. Look around you. You are all the same so intent on your anger, violence and warfare that you are trapped.

Look behind you. See the faces and feel the love from your ancestors and all those who came after you. You have trapped them and their lives are also filled with anger, and with longing and sadness and despair that you cannot know of their love for you.

Your memories of old times, fights, anger and bloodshed are only that. You can never win and change the past. It is solid like me. It cannot and will not yield. It is one of the truths we live by. It is absurd to relive it every day expecting a different outcome. It cannot change."

I pointed behind them and the kings slowly turned around. It was as if they came out of a trance as they saw for the first time the lights that were the souls of their loved ones. Some of them stood, arms stretched out towards the kings, others remained preying, silently beseeching them.

"See how your family, your soul family is waiting for you. They have waited thousands of years. Would you punish them to wait thousands more? How long will you have them wait? How long until you feel their love?"

One by one the kings shook their heads. I saw one rub his huge hands across his face, smeared in muck. Another stood up and looked from the sword still in his grasp then over towards the souls, then back again before he laid it down. Another couple did the same with their spears. The words had reached them, and without even a glance in my direction, they stood and then in unison they stepped down from the stone thrones. They walked slowly towards where their loved ones waited, no longer wailing and weeping. Instead their faces were full of hope, and beamed with love and expectation.

With every step forward they became more transparent, so that by the time they reached the edge of the chamber, to the place where their descendants' souls sparkled and glistened, they too had become the same. I had to hold my eyes up to protect them from the brightness of the light that had burst from behind them like a star. I had a glimpse of the souls merging into one, all anger from the kings left in the past forever. I wondered what effect it could possibly have.

Chapter Twenty-Four

I woke up outside Newgrange, leaning against the large standing stone. Relief flooded through me. The air was fresh and cold, icy droplets hung in the air, and the light was fading. A weak sun had begun its descent behind the hill. I was out and seeing the sky again for the first time in what seemed ages. I pulled my hands through my hair, fixing it high on my head. Tentatively I stood up, a bit stiff but not as sore as I'd expected. I smoothed out my coat. My bag was still where I'd left it, I opened it and found my purse and mobile phone in the side pocket.

I flicked on the phone, entered my code and checked the time. It was exactly seventeen minutes after Martha had left me outside the monument. Exactly the same time it took the sun beam to travel across the chamber at the solstice. It chirped with messages and alerts. I had seventeen missed calls. I quickly scrolled through them and the list of texts. One of the numbers had an international code I didn't recognise. I held my breath as I clicked it open. I knew before I read it that it was from Guy.

"Hey Kirsty from Lanark. It was such a pleasure to meet you. I've really been thinking about what you said about the sonar technology and how it might be affecting the marine life. I'm heading north. You gave me lots to think about. Would be great to talk when you get a minute. Enjoy Ireland!"

The same number was on my missed call list. I dialled my voice mail code, then pulled my gloves back on, as the chill from the day started to hit me. His lovely voice was instantly familiar. I was transported back to the ferry journey that had started this whole adventure. He'd left the message five minutes before.

"Hey Kirsty, can you let me know you are ok? I've really been thinking about what you said, and I've decided to pull my technology until I've had some more time to analyse my results. So I wanted you to know that as of a few minutes ago, the sonar is off. We'll see if that makes a difference."

I leaned back against the stone, feeling its power and the low beat from the ground beneath. It had worked for the sonar. I had a feeling that would be the start of good changes for us all.

Sleet blew into my face, as sharp as glass, and I felt that snow would soon follow. The wind whistled around the stones and I took that as time to leave, walking back down towards the road careful to avoid any faery rings. I wouldn't take that risk again. The gate clicked shut behind me, Martha would lock up later. I knew I had time to visit the white house at the bottom of the hill before it got dark. Turning towards it, I pushed my hands deep inside my pockets to stay warm. I would see my grandfather soon, and perhaps hear about my dad.

Walking down the lane, I was comforted by the bleating of sheep from the fields on either side of me, a mist hung low on the surface. I breathed deeply, filling my lungs with damp air. The road curved round some large rocks, I could hear water and within a few steps I crossed a small stone bridge. My feet crunched across its gritty surface. Pausing for a moment half way across I leaned over to rest my arms on the low wall, watching the clear, shallow water below me. Peering down I could just about make out small stones sitting in the shallows, and saw bubbles of air as fish broke the surface. I looked around me, really appreciating everything I could see, and took a breath. Everything felt calm and quiet after my experience.

With my breath back, I turned to follow the road, and I heard the now familiar tapping of a cane and shuffling footsteps. The old man appeared beside me. He was dressed differently. More modern, wearing a dark water-proof jacket, a woollen cap and thick gloves. He looked dressed for the elements. His hair sat over his collar but was not as long as it was earlier. He was the same but different. He smiled at me in recognition. There was some-thing in his expression, in the twinkle in his eyes. He was looking at me with respect, I was no longer the student. I had endured and I had survived. I remembered what he had said about walking the labyrinth, and wanted to know more. Most importantly, I wanted to know if the stones were safe and if the whales would be ok now that the sonar was turned off.

We stood together for a moment, his gloved hand reached over and covered mine. And in that gesture I knew that everything was as it had to be. He hadn't said a word and I realised that sometimes we don't need to speak, sometimes we need to trust ourselves with what we're feeling deep inside.

He squeezed my hand and thoughts of my grandfather came into my mind. I had a sudden urge to get to the white house and see him. The old man smiled into my eyes, and I could feel the pride he had for me, before he turned away and vanished into the mist.

I felt invigorated by his presence and walked quickly down hill, soon arriving at a high hedge. I followed it around, my fingers touching the closely packed leaves. A bubble of anticipation filled me up and threatened to burst out of me. Finally I was about to meet my grandfather and find out more about my dad.

Through a gap in the hedge I glimpsed the white house for the first time. It was a big imposing house, sat back off the road. Lamps behind the leaded glass windows shone out into the gathering gloom. I walked over a white gritted driveway, it reminded me of the quartz front of Newgrange. A couple of wide steps took me to a big red painted doorway, plants sat on either side of a small porch area. Everything looked polished and very well looked after. I pressed a bell, and listened as it sounded somewhere deep inside the house. I imagined my grandfather sitting in one of the rooms, reading a newspaper, hearing the bell and taking his time, folding his paper, walking slowly to the door and what he would say when he saw me standing there. No doubt he would know that I was coming.

The door opened quickly and a young woman stood smiling at me. Her eyebrow raised in enquiry, she obviously wasn't expecting me. She wore a lilac tunic like a nurse would wear. She looked tired, and harassed. I smiled at her and gave my name and asked to see my grandfather. She asked for his name, which surprised me, and didn't seem to have a clue any idea of who I was. She opened the door wider to let me enter into a wide hallway. It had a sort of institutional smell, like a hospital. She walked over towards a wide dark oak desk, and asked me to sign in and asked for my grandfather's name again.

As I leaned over to write my name and fill in my grand-father's in the appropriate column, my relation to him, and my arrival time the penny was starting to drop. I was in a care home, not my grandfather's house. I hadn't real-ised that. As soon as she knew who I wanted to visit and glanced over to see that I had written granddaughter, her attitude completely changed.

"Your Billy's grand-daughter! Of course I can see the resemblance now. Welcome, welcome, I haven't seen you before have I? Let me take you to his room. He's much brighter today than he's been for ages. His room has a lovely view of the gardens and up the hillside to Newgrange. We wouldn't dare put him anywhere else!"

She chattered on as she walked quickly up the grand staircase, motioning for me to follow her. A huge stained glass window towered above us. Multi coloured faeries and other supernatural creatures danced around the bottom of a hill, and along the top there was a circle of empty stone thrones, surrounding a temple that looked like Newgrange. I couldn't help but shiver as I walked past, and followed her along the panelled hallway, our feet sank deep into the green carpet. She was oblivious to my grow-ing unease. My palms sweated and I unfastened my coat, the temperature had been set incredibly high. The smell of furniture polish mingled with antiseptic. The lights were low and I could hear the muted sounds of music and tele-visions from behind doors as we walked along.

At the end of the hallway she stopped outside a large mahogany door, and tapped softly, listening for a moment before she pushed it open. Nodding for me to enter in front of her. I heard the door click behind me and I took a deep breath as I looked around the room. I was looking towards a big bay window, green velvet curtains draped the stunning view of Newgrange, lit up and glowing at the top of the hill.

In front of the window, set up so the occupant could always enjoy the magical view, was a hospital style bed. I could smell antiseptic and the sweet smell of custard and soft foods, as well as a faded floral fragrance.

I walked across the thick carpeted floor, and sat down on one of the two empty seats before I chanced a glimpse at the occupant. Part of me hoped that the nurse was mistaken and she'd taken me to someone else's room. The other part of me knew that this was coming.

In the bed lay the old druid, or at least someone who looked so like him they could have been twins. His white hair was long, his face smoothed in sleep. His eyes closed, his hands rested on top of the crisp white sheets tightly tucked around him. On one hand I saw the edges of a blue tattoo of a snake peaking from the edge of his striped pyjamas. A walking frame sat on the other side of the bed, with a walking stick leaning beside it. There was a bed table, and upon it lay the remnants of lunch, it looked like strawberry custard, a plastic spoon lay in the mush like something a baby would leave.

There was no doubt. This was the old man I'd seen today, and the old druid who I'd met at the temple in Glasgow, and the one who'd led me into the chamber. The question for me, was how had he done it?

I leaned over and grasped the old hand closest to me. Suddenly overcome with sadness, I sniffed back tears. All of the experience had been about meeting my grandfather and I'd known him for days. I had no idea how that had happened but it had been him. I knew it, but what would I learn from him now?

The door open behind me, and I heard the rustle as someone walked in to the room and padded over towards me.

"Kirsty?" an older female voice asked.

I turned round, nodding, blinking away tears.

"How are you? Your grandfather knew you were coming. He's been calling your name out for days now."

"So he is able to speak? I wasn't sure when I saw him like this?"

I looked at the woman closer, she was in her early sixties and also dressed in a uniform. She wore a name plate on her chest which said her name was Anne.

"Do you remember this place? You used to come with your dad a long time ago, just after your grandfather had his first stroke. Do you remember? You haven't changed a bit."

"Not really. Can you tell me more about him?"

"He's had a series of strokes over the last twenty years or so. The last one was about three months ago but he's doing well. We haven't heard much from him recently but the last week or so he's been saying your name, all the time. Knowing what he's like, I knew you were coming."

She looked at him affectionately and patted his shoulder, before leaving the room. I heard the door close softly behind her.

My grandfather moved a little in his sleep, and I moved closer, rubbing the back of his hand. My fingers hovered over the blue marks etched on his skin, I was dying to touch it. When I looked back at him his eyes were open and bright. He silently mouthed my name.

His mouth moved into a lop-sided grimace and I worried that he was in pain, but then I realised that he was trying to smile.

"It's ok Granda. It's ok." I tried to reassure him, his old title came easily and naturally to mind. "Can I get you anything?"

He glanced towards his bedside cabinet, but I didn't know what he wanted. It was crammed with personal stuff, I noticed photograph frames and a little brass clock. He looked at a plastic beaker on the side table and I offered him that, he nodded and I held the straw to his mouth so he could suck it. As I bent over to help him I felt suddenly sad and ashamed. All of these years I should have been helping him and instead I'd left it to others. I made a vow that I'd take care of him. His hand reached up and touched my cheek and for a moment I could feel the power of him. We looked deep into each other's eyes and I knew I wasn't to be sorry. That's not what he wanted.

I remembered that feeling I'd had at the bridge, that we didn't need to talk to understand each other. I hoped there was a way for me to find out about my dad. I really wanted to meet him again. That fleeting phone call, the unopened letters, I had to connect with him and find out more. I hoped that the stones were safe and the whales, but was that enough? I had a feeling that there would be more to do and I shivered again, a little fleck of blue light flashed at the edge of my vision. My granda rubbed my hand as if to comfort me, and I remembered an earlier time from visiting the house, but he'd been in a different room. He smiled and I knew he had helped me find that memory

The door opened and Anne came back into the room.

"Did you get your message Kirsty?"

"What message?"

She leaned past me and pulled out a postcard from behind Granda's possessions. That must have been what he was trying to show me.

"This came for you yesterday. Well it's addressed to both of you but I've read it to this man a hundred times, haven't I Billy?"

She laughed and handed it to me. On the front was a coloured map. I held it up to the light to see that it was from the Orkney Islands, where Grizelle said she was headed. The map was of Skara Brae, an ancient archaeological site, off the north coast of Scotland.

I turned it over, scrawled across the card was the same writing from those old letters I'd found at home. It was addressed to me in such a familiar hand that had possibly written my name from before I was even born.

It was signed simply Dad. My breath caught in my throat and I felt my grandfathers' eyes follow me as I walked to the window better able to read in its light, but also to attempt to hide my shocked expression.

Kirsty. Welcome home. Well done my girl. I'm proud of you. I need you to come to Skara Brae. We'll catch up properly here. There's so much to tell. I'll see you soon. The Stone of Destiny needs us.

About The Author

KT Finegan lives on the Ayrshire coast where she writes and delivers workshops on spiritual development, and offers intuitive coaching. Please email info@ktfinegan.com if you would like more information, or want to know when the final instalment of the Guardians of the Stone is released.